T0114540

$\mathcal{W}hite$ is
BORING

SEYMOUR GREBOW

authorHOUSE®

AuthorHouse™
1663 Liberty Drive
Bloomington, IN 47403
www.authorhouse.com
Phone: 1 (800) 839-8640

This is a work of fiction. All of the characters, names, incidents,
organizations, and dialogue in this novel are either the products
of the author's imagination or are used fictitiously.

© 2016 Seymour Grebow. All rights reserved.

No part of this book may be reproduced, stored in a retrieval system, or
transmitted by any means without the written permission of the author.

Published by AuthorHouse 07/01/2016

ISBN: 978-1-5246-1711-0 (sc)
ISBN: 978-1-5246-1710-3 (e)

Print information available on the last page.

Any people depicted in stock imagery provided by Thinkstock are models,
and such images are being used for illustrative purposes only.
Certain stock imagery © Thinkstock.

This book is printed on acid-free paper.

Because of the dynamic nature of the Internet, any web addresses or
links contained in this book may have changed since publication and
may no longer be valid. The views expressed in this work are solely those
of the author and do not necessarily reflect the views of the publisher,
and the publisher hereby disclaims any responsibility for them.

A well-dressed woman walked into the Palm Beach Eminent paint store.

An elderly man, leaning heavily on a cane, approached her with a big smile of greeting. "Welcome. My name is Norman. May I help you?"

"Yes, please. I wish to paint the interior of my home, and I decided I want it all white."

"Well, could I please ask you to step over to our extensive wall of the latest colors in fashion today? White is boring."

Chapter 1

It was another cold day in December. The temperature was twelve degrees. Norman could hear the snowplows trying to clear the roads. The snow was more than a foot deep, and it was still snowing.

Fran drove up to the front door, blew the horn, and waited. Norman did not appear. She blew the horn again and waited. Finally she got out of the car, reached into the backseat, took out several large grocery bags, and walked with difficulty to the snow-covered front door.

She opened the door and called to Norman, "Please come and help me."

"Not now, Fran. The president is about to make a speech."

Fran made three trips to bring in the large bags and dropped them on the floor. She removed her woolen scarf and wet hat. Fran sat on a bench to take off her wet boots, and then she carried the bags into the kitchen. She put them on the table and began putting everything away.

Norman walked into the kitchen. "Wow, what a great speech the president made." He looked through the bags. "Where are the prunes? You forgot to buy prunes. You know I need prunes."

Fran gave a sigh of resignation but said nothing as Norman returned to the living room. She went upstairs to change into more comfortable clothes. She made the bed, piled the laundry into a basket, and carried it downstairs to the laundry room. Fran prepared tuna sandwiches for lunch and made a pot of fresh coffee.

"Norman, lunch is ready."

There was no answer.

As she ate, she looked out the kitchen window. It was still snowing.

"Norman," she called again.

"Not now!" he shouted. "The bases are loaded, and it's two outs."

Fran walked into the living room and turned off the TV. "Norman, you listen to me. I did not complain when you told me that this was the only house we could afford as you were building your business. I agreed when our children entered college and then graduate school that we should pay everything so they would not incur large debt. I went along with you. After a lifetime in the retail paint business as a dealer for the Carson Forester Paint Manufacturing Company, you were too tired to continue the business and sold the store. I didn't complain when my friend Hannah and her husband, the accountant, bought a large, new ranch house with the master bedroom and bath on the ground floor. Or when we play mahjong in Ceciel's enclosed sunroom with a permanent card table and matching chairs, while I have a folding table with four folding chairs that I set up in the living room. I always consoled myself with the thought that this would be the time for us to be together."

"Fran, you are a 100 percent right. This is our time. I have a surprise for you. Tomorrow we have an appointment with an agent to discuss a reverse mortgage. You can fix this house any way you wish."

"Norman, I still love you, but I am not going to die in this house. I am sick of the ice, the snow, the freezing cold, and the heavy clothes. We are selling this house and moving to Florida."

A month later they were settled in a beautiful, ground-floor condo in a senior community in Boca Raton.

"I'm going to become an artist," declared Norman.

"I'm going to attend lectures and play mahjong in the clubhouse," declared Fran.

The next morning Norman shopped at Michael's for art supplies, loading a shopping cart with acrylic paint of all colors, including white and black; a dozen different-sized brushes; and several instruction books.

Every evening they relaxed in the screened-in terrace, enjoying the warm weather. Every morning Norman was busy removing the backs of the pictures they brought with them, turning the picture around and creating works of art on the reverse side. Many of his ideas came from magazines. Soon his original works of art covered every wall in their home.

"Now what? I think I'll join the village fishing club," said Norman. "I brought all my rods and equipment from the North."

"That's great," replied Fran. "When you were younger, you always enjoyed fishing. Just don't expect to clean any fish in my kitchen."

After another month Norman was drinking a lot of coffee, listening to the same news over and over on the TV, falling asleep in the afternoons, and complaining about how tired he was.

One afternoon he said, "You know, Fran, for me, somehow now when I get out of bed in the morning, the best part of the day is over."

Fran looked at him. "So do something about it. Just don't follow me around and interfere in my activities."

Early the next morning, Norman dressed and told Fran as he left, "I am going to find a part-time job. Enough sitting around and complaining."

On entering the Palm Beach Eminent paint store, Norman's old instincts welled up in his brain. He suddenly felt alive again. "Good morning. May I speak to the owner please?"

"Sure," replied a well-dressed, attractive young woman. "Follow me."

The Palm Beach Eminent paint store was also an authorized dealer for the Carson Forester Paint Manufacturer Company. It had been purchased by two couples who had relocated to Boca Raton and financed by a good friend already living in Boca. Reza and Victor Sanchez, brother and sister, were smart, hardworking, and determined to succeed. The business prospered and was now a major dealer of the Carson Forester Paint Company.

"Hello, I am Reza. How can I help you?"

"Thank you, Reza. I would like the opportunity to work here part time."

After an hour of conversation, they agreed he'd work eleven o'clock to three o'clock three days a week.

Norman happily settled into a familiar routine. Customers quickly started calling for appointments and lined up at the counter to discuss and seek advice about their painting projects. Norman's knowledge of the Carson

Forester products was a plus. His customers trusted his advice about the different finishes. Norman explained patiently how to accomplish beautiful results. His color selections, suggestions, and combinations were amazing.

Reza, an unbelievably smart, charming, and sophisticated businessperson, marveled at his knowledge and the way he enjoyed dealing with people. Arnold, a young contractor, struck up a great friendship with Norman, and Norman somewhat became a mentor to him.

Everyone realized Norman's difficulty in walking—as he relied heavily on a cane—was a concern. They all watched over him constantly, not allowing him to lift anything heavy.

Early one morning, Norman said, "Reza, I'd like to discuss something with you and Victor when you both have time."

"Sure, Norman. Victor will be here in a few minutes. When you see him, come into my office."

Victor bounced in. "What's up, Norman?"

"I want to talk to you both about an idea I have for a new interior wall paint. I think it might have some promise. I'd like permission to stay in the mixing room after work to test my idea. Also I'd need access to the paint bases and colorants. I may ask Arnold to assist me. In return, if my idea is successful, I'd like us all to be partners."

"Wow, Norman, that was a long speech," declared Victor. "Reza and I have tremendous confidence in your ability. I'm sure you know *mi casa es su casa*."

During the ensuing months, Reza and Victor were amazed at the high level of Norman's ideas and powers of concentration. Arnold was a great help with the mathematics and keeping track of the ingredients for the formula.

Norman called one morning. "Reza, Arnold and I are really close to final testing and are at a crucial stage."

"That's great! Just let us know when you're ready."

Several weeks later, on June 4, Norman called excitedly to Reza and Victor, "Could you both come into the mixing room? We're on our way to a great invention. Arnold, would you please set up the drawdowns? We are going to demonstrate a new product I believe will start a revolution in interior decorating. But until we receive a patent, secrecy is critical. We have named it MajDec, an abbreviation for magic decorating.

"So here it is. We have perfected a process where the same color in daylight will change to a deeper color with electric light. Also the finish at night will give off a soft glow and a very happy feeling. But there's still a lot of testing to be accomplished."

After they viewed the sample drawdowns, Arnold stepped outside and held up the samples. Then he returned to the room, and under the electric light, the colors slowly turned darker and took on a soft glow.

That evening, a meeting was held in Reza's spacious townhome. Present were Reza and her husband, Juan; Victor and his wife, Rosetta; Arnold and Rebecca; and Norman and Fran. The greetings were cordial yet reserved. Everyone sat quietly waiting.

Arnold glanced at everyone before turning to the subject at hand. "I'm sure you have already heard we've invented a product so unique that it could change the interior painting market." He explained the details of MajDec and then asked, "So how do we proceed?"

Arnold shared, "Norman and I hope that we four couples will form a partnership to decide how best to market MajDec."

Everyone was deep in thought, and then the questions came. "Can we market this ourselves? Are we able to finance this? Should we seek a financial partner?"

Victor spoke up, "I believe we should discuss this with our attorney."

They all agreed, and a week later, the company attorney had prepared partnership agreements and completed and submitted all patent applications.

One of the richest and most successful companies in America was the Carson Forester Company, manufacturers of high-quality paints and coatings. Mr. Carson Forester founded the company. He was reputed to be the seventh-richest man in America, though not all his wealth came from this company. However, the privately owned company would not divulge any financial information. Carson was now semi-active, holding the title of chairman of the board of directors. Full authority was in the capable leadership of his only son, Adam.

Chapter 2

It was an unusually warm and sunny day in May. Adam Forester and his wife Vivian, the only heir to the Kendall real estate empire, were both very excited and happy about their trip. They flew in the company jet to Philadelphia to attend the graduation of their son, Randolph, or as everyone in the family called him, Randy.

Also present on the jet was Vanessa, Adam's sister, and her husband, Franklin Bailey. Unfortunately their daughter Alexis, a senior at Boston University, was unable to attend as she was in the midst of finals. Randy was to receive his master's degree from Wharton. Arriving separately was Carson and Eleanor Forester, Randy's grandmother and grandfather. It was a very happy occasion for the family, especially for the grandparents, as this was the only heir to carry on the Forester name.

It was Monday morning in the executive suite of the Carson Forester Company, and CEO Scott Peterson pressed a buzzer. "Maria, please arrange a phone call with the owners of the Palm Beach Eminent paint store."

"Yes, sir. Right away," she told him. Once on the phone, she continued, "Good morning. I am Maria. This is the executive office of Mr. Scott Peterson. He wishes to speak to the owner, please."

"Hello, Maria. My name is Reza Sanchez. I am an owner."

"Thank you, Mrs. Sanchez. Please hold."

"Mrs. Sanchez, I am Scott Peterson, CEO of Carson Forester. I have become aware of a new product your company has invented. I cannot divulge how I received this information, but I'd like to meet with you to discuss us exploring some type of joint venture. Also I have been informed that your company enjoys an outstanding record of purchases from us."

"Thank you, Mr. Peterson. Four couples are involved in this product. I will certainly discuss your offer and call you back as soon as possible."

"Hello, Victor. Please return to the store immediately and meet me in the mixing room."

"Reza, I'll be there in fifteen minutes."

Soon after, Reza explained, "Guys, a new development has emerged. I received a phone call from Scott Peterson. I am sure you all know who he is. Information has already leaked out about our invention. He wishes to meet with us to discuss a joint venture."

Arnold jumped to his feet. "That's great! Carson Forester can provide what we need."

Then Norman asked, "What is your opinion, Victor?"

He replied, "We have nothing to lose by hearing his proposal."

"I will call him now," replied Reza. "Because we are together, you will hear our conversation."

After a few moments, they heard, "Good morning, Mr. Peterson's office. This is Maria."

"Hello, Maria. This is Reza Sanchez. I am returning Mr. Peterson's call."

"Please hold," Maria stated.

Scott answered his private line, "So what is the answer?"

"We have agreed to meet with you."

"Excellent. I will have the company chopper pick you up Wednesday morning at 9:00 a.m. and bring you to my office in Atlanta."

"Mr. Peterson, we have four couples involved. Can the helicopter accommodate eight passengers?"

"Absolutely," he replied, "and you will be returned to Boca by late afternoon. Maria will make all the arrangements, and I will see you Wednesday."

⊰⊱⊱⊰

As a huge helicopter landed in the yard of the store, the pilot jumped out. "Are you all ready?"

In flight, everyone was deep in contemplation. An hour later, everyone was ushered into the executive suite.

"Good morning. I am Maria, Mr. Peterson's private secretary."

Reza smiled and extended her hand. "Good morning to you also. *Que vai acontecer.*"

Maria replied, "*No va a ser una conversion facil.*"

Scott Peterson rose from behind the desk. "Please be seated. Maria, send in a stenographer to record our conversation." Without smiling, he continued, "Let's start with the premise that you do not have any manufacturing facilities. You also do not have a network of dealers. You do not have a marketing department, an advertising setup, and a lot more that is required for success. But most important is the amount of money you will need, and let's not overlook that your invention is formulated in our satin finish enamel."

Victor stood. "Mr. Peterson, everything you say is true, but what we have is the patent on a revolutionary product that will shake up and amaze every decorator and painting contractor and, most important, the demands from the public."

Arnold also stood. "It's true that it will take a lot of money and hard work to market ourselves. Also, if we have to, we can reformulate on another company's product, even though that would be many more months of testing."

Reza stood alongside Victor and Arnold. "Mr. Peterson, we would agree to turn over all patent and formulas to Carson Forester for a payment of four dollars for each gallon sold."

An unsmiling Peterson stood up. "That's a little too generous. I had two dollars in mind."

After another hour of back-and-forth discussion with no agreement, Peterson stood up and thanked everyone for coming. "I have decided to pass on this opportunity." He sat down.

"Hello, Grandpa. This is Randy. First, let me thank you and Grandma for the very generous graduation gift."

Carson replied, "You are very welcome! We are proud of your degree."

"Grandpa, I have to speak to you about a business proposal."

"Absolutely. I expect to be in Atlanta starting next week for a director's meeting. Meet me in my office next to the boardroom."

"Thanks, Grandpa, and give my love to Grandma."

On Monday morning Randy was waiting for Grandpa in his private office.

After a huge hug, Randy immediately said, "Grandpa, I am sure you are aware that Scott Peterson turned down the joint venture offer with a group from Boca that has invented an interesting new product."

Carson replied, "I was not informed. Please give me details."

Speaking calmly, Randy related the details.

"So Randy, why are you telling me this?"

"Because," replied Randy, "I want to negotiate an agreement with them and manufacture the product. What I need is your approval and start-up money. I googled a copy of the patents. It requires very technical heating and cooling equipment, plus everything else. Also I would need manufacturing space and …"

"Hold on, Randy," exclaimed Carson. "Let me get your father in here."

Randy was approximately five-foot-eleven with broad shoulders and sandy-colored hair that refused to stay in place. He had handsome features with deep brown eyes that sparkled when he smiled or laughed but turned deep bark brown when making important decisions. He mingled easily with his fellow students at the Greenwood Academy for Boys in Atlanta. He was a straight-A student and an A player on the golf team.

When he was a student, on every Friday night, the Academy hosted a student dance held in the Greenwood Academy for Girls gymnasium. Both principals chaperoned. The band was playing the fox-trot.

Randy, with the usual air of authority, walked up to the young lady, smiled, and asked, "Would you care to dance?"

She smiled back and nodded. He took her hand, and they walked to the center of the floor, where he circled her waist with his arm and led her into a smooth rhythm to the beat of the music. He tenderly and expertly turned her. He guided her around the floor, holding her closer. They flowed with the music.

Once the song ended, Randy, still holding her hand, said, "That was really great. Thank you."

He stepped over to the bandleader and spoke in a low whisper. He approached another young lady, and as the band began to play the beautiful Blue Danube waltz, he asked, "Would you care to dance?"

She smiled. "Yes, I would."

He circled her waist, held her close, and led her into a tender waltz. They swayed, dipped, and whirled to the beautiful music. Circling the floor, the young lady felt as if her feet were not touching the floor as he gracefully led her whirling to the music.

When it ended, he held her hand. "You are a terrific dance partner."

"Thank you."

As on other Friday nights, he danced with many of the girls and left them all breathless.

And on Sunday mornings, he and his father had a 7:00 a.m. tee-off time at the club. Most mornings it was hole play and a lot of good-natured ribbing and laughing. It was a very special time for them. In the afternoon, if his cousin Tom were available, they had a serious tennis match with the club pro watching every move and correcting, urging them to be better players.

Randy entered George Washington University in Washington, DC, as a freshman. As he moved into his dormitory room, he was calm because he was confident that his application for admittance would be approved. He was immediately recruited to be on the golf team. In his dorm room, his golf clubs were always leaning against the headboard by his bed, and along the wall was his tennis bag.

But he was a serious student. Every day that he went to class or a lecture, he wore slacks with a sharp crease, a white shirt and a tie, and a matching sports jacket. After four years, he had maintained a 4.0 grade point average. He was on the phone with his mother at least three times a week and with his grandfather at least twice a week. He had no time for dating.

After several hours of discussion, Randy's father, Adam, agreed to move some of the manufacturing from the Jacksonville, Florida, plant to either Dallas or Newark plants.

"Randy, that will give you almost half of the Jacksonville plant building. The other half will continue manufacturing regular products."

Grandpa chimed in, "Randy, set up a new division of the company, and we will fund it from my personal discretionary account."

With hugging and kissing all around, Randy left very excited and called Reza.

"Hello, this is Reza Sanchez. How can I help you?"

"Mrs. Sanchez, I am Randy Forester. I am calling regarding the meeting you had with Mr. Peterson. I want to prepare an agreement for a payment of four dollars a gallon to you."

"Mr. Forester, I appreciate your offer. Please come to our store, and we will review your agreement."

Two days later, all contracts were signed. A separate agreement was that Randy would hire two chemists that he would pay to help in the testing and completing the formulas. On Monday morning, the chemists, Chrissy and Mark, arrived in Boca. Norman informed them that he wanted three hundred colors, and so far they had finalized one hundred and twenty-five. Randy sent a construction crew to enlarge and modernize the area into a full-service laboratory.

Meanwhile activity in Jacksonville was a blur with building new partitions, moving walls, purchasing special equipment, hiring, planning, and consulting newly hired engineers. It was organized confusion with hiring heating and cooling specialists, office personnel, and a lot more. Randy, driving in a golf cart, was all over, directing. He was totally obsessed with the project.

"Hello, boss. I am sorry to startle you. I am your new assistant, Paula."

"Really?" replied Randy. "Since when?"

"Right now," answered Paula.

"Yes, boss. My name is Paula. I have hired a driver for you and leased a Lincoln SUV. Meet Sam. He is your driver."

"Okay, Paula. You're on. Start by organizing all payroll records for all the new employees. Inform everyone that you are my new assistant. Also do not call me boss. My name is Randy and arrange a flight for me to Atlanta. Next get me a copy of all Forester dealers. You figure out how."

In Atlanta, Randy was working out the printing of the color cards, color decks, and brochures. The next day, his father walked into the plant on a surprise visit.

"Hi, Pop," greeted Randy.

He and Adam kissed and hugged.

"What a welcome surprise. How is Mom? I have been so busy that I have not had time to call her. Pop, let me give you a tour, but first I want you to meet my very able assistant, Paula." Adam gave her a wink.

"Hello, Paula. You and I have had several conversations, and I appreciate you keeping my visit today a complete surprise."

"Okay, you two conspirators, hop in the golf cart. We will stop at the loading docks. Here, we will receive all the ingredients. The conveyors will bring them to a loft, where everything will be gravity-fed into the proper vats. We will set up hundreds of separate mixing vats and feeder pipes. Each color must be kept separate. We also manufacture our special primer in this area. Moving along, these central panels carefully regulate the heating and cooling as the formula requires. This must be monitored closely to produce MajDec."

"Now in this area is the time controls. Each ingredient must be timed precisely in the intermixing process. Okay, now these feeder pipes pump the finished paint to fill the containers and move it on to the conveyor belt to be labeled, put on panels, stamped with the dealer's name, and placed on to the loading dock where we have tractor trailers waiting. At a later date, I would like you to meet Norman, whose genius invented this entire process. Dad, as for now, all billing and payments are handled in Atlanta."

Adam was so impressed by what he was witnessing. He almost forgot his surprise gift.

"Randy, I have taken a delivery of a new jet, and instead of trading in the present company jet, I am going to give it to you to make it easier for you to travel."

"Wow, Pop! That's really great! And Paula, find us a pilot."

"Yes, sir. It's already done. Sam is also a competent pilot since I was notified of this before I hired him."

"Well done, Randy. I have to leave now. Sam will bring me to Atlanta and then return. Now listen to me. This coming weekend, I will be going with Mom, Aunt Vanessa, and Uncle Franklin to the Breakers Hotel in Palm Beach to relax and play golf. We would really like you to join us. We are scheduled to arrive there Thursday afternoon."

"Pop, thanks. That would be wonderful. I could use a break," exclaimed Randy.

Chapter 3

On Thursday afternoon, also arriving at the Breakers Hotel were Dr. Charles Vanderbrook, his wife Carol, and their only daughter Sandra, also known as Sandy. She lived the privileged life and went to the finest schools. Sandy would graduate from George Washington University in D.C this year and was accepted to law school there. Tall and blonde, she was tan with an athletic body that every woman envied and every male had to sneak a peek. She was on the golf and tennis team, where she excelled in both. She always wanted to be a lawyer and held a straight A grade point average. She was greatly loved and protected, especially by her older brother, Dr. Byron Vanderbrook, a skilled orthopedic surgeon.

The elder Dr. Vanderbook, author of many scientific papers, would be a major speaker Friday night on the advances in robotic surgery. This was the annual gathering of the top surgeons in the United States. With him was Byron and his wife Dina. Both doctors had homes in Rumson, New Jersey, and offices in Manhattan.

As the Vanderbrooks were relaxing in the hotel lobby, greeting many of the arriving doctors and wives, two limos with the Foresters and Baileys arrived. Randy arrived a few minutes later in a rented convertible. Because so many guests were arriving, the lobby was crowded.

"Adam, why don't we relax here for a while until the lines at the counter are shorter," asked Vivian.

Adam called the concierge over to discuss tee times and dinner plans. Randy was busy observing the gathering crowd. Suddenly, sitting a few feet away was the most beautiful girl he had ever seen. She was chattering and laughing apparently with other members of her family. He could not take his eyes off her, and in a startling moment, Sandy must have realized he was looking at her and smiled at him. She turned away and continued her conversation. Randy realized he was having difficulty breathing.

Dinner in the grand dining room was bedlam but enjoyable with good-natured and lively conversation. Vanessa realized that Randy was distracted as he casually looked around the room. Suddenly he stood and excused himself.

Without hesitation, he approached the Vanderbrook table. "Please excuse my inappropriate intrusion. My name is Randy Forester, and I could not contain myself. My family is also staying here. Would I be out of line by asking you," he asked, looking at Sandy, "if you would consider having an after-dinner drink with me?"

An awkward silence ensued. Randy blushed and turned to leave when Sandra smiled.

"I will meet you later in the bar."

Both Sandra's and Randy's family kept looking at each other as discreetly as possible, not believing what had just transpired.

Randy selected a booth with a clear view of the door. He waited eagerly and was very nervous. "Am I nuts? What did I do? This is not my style. I must be crazy." But once he saw her entering with her brother, he knew this girl was special.

"Randy, please say hello to my brother Byron."

"I am pleased to meet you, sir. May I explain? I realize my actions were very aggressive, but I assure you I have been brought up to always be a gentleman. When I saw your sister, I just had to meet her."

Byron replied, "I know of your family and the many charities that your grandfather has funded. It is just that we are very protective of our Sandy. So don't stay up too late, Sis."

Looking at each other across the table, Randy was trying to act cool. Then they both started talking at once, telling college stories, discussing family, and completely forgetting to order a drink.

"Oh no!" exclaimed Sandy. "It's after midnight. I'm playing golf tomorrow morning. Do you play golf, Randy?"

"Yes," he replied, "I played a little in college."

"Well, Byron, Dina, and I have a ten o'clock tee time. As we are three, how about joining us?"

"That would be great," said Randy, beaming.

After getting into bed, this special girl kept him wide-awake. At nine thirty the next morning, Randy was sitting on a bench at the first tee with his golf clubs beside him, waiting anxiously. He was upset that he had not brought more fashionable golf clothes and a newer pair of shoes and was wearing an old baseball cap. His parents, Vanessa, and Franklin arrived in a golf cart for a tee time of nine forty-five.

"Hi, Randy," his father exclaimed. "You told us you were not going to play golf and just relax."

As he hugged and kissed everyone, especially his mother, he replied, "The girl I met last night, Sandy, invited me to join her, her brother, and his wife. We have a ten o'clock tee time, and I am very nervous."

His mother gave him a big reassuring smile, and his father patted him on the back and said, "Go for it. She is beautiful."

A few minutes later, Sandy drove up alone in a golf cart. Following her were Byron and Dina.

Sandy jumped out and ran over to the group. "Hi, everybody! I'd like all of us to meet! This is my brother Byron and his wife Dina."

Randy could not believe what he was seeing. Sandy was dressed in a beautiful, all-white golf outfit, except for a short skirt with pink underpants and a pink and white cap.

Seeing her son speechless, Vivian spoke up, "We are Randy's parents. I am Vivian, this is my husband Adam, and in the other cart is Adam's sister Vanessa and her husband Franklin. We are pleased to meet you all."

Over the loudspeaker could be heard, "The Forester foursome on the tee, please."

Byron smiled. "We'll be following you. Please try not to play too slowly!"

That elicited a laugh from all.

While Randy was securing his bag to the cart, Sandy was eyeing his bag and clubs. "Your clubs are fantastic, and you have a professional bag. You even have Forester engraved on both sides. Very impressive."

Randy, still in a slight daze, replied, "These are custom-fitted clubs. I went to Connecticut with my Grandpa Carson. This was my graduation present."

Over the loudspeaker came, "The Vanderbrook foursome on the tee, please."

Sandy jumped into the passenger seat. "Would you drive, please?"

"Sure," replied Randy, now fully in control again.

Byron selected a driver and placed his ball on the tee. He wiggled the club a few times and sent the ball flying straight down the fairway.

"Beautiful!" Randy teed up next. He gave a few practice swings of his driver and gave the ball a powerful shot. It also flew down the fairway, out of sight.

"You rat!" shouted Sandy.

"Oh, yeah. I played a little golf in college," Randy replied with a sly wink.

"You are a rat. You tricked me!" shouted Sandy.

As Byron and Randy were standing at the ladies tee, Byron said, "This morning I walked into the pro shop to see what's new in golf equipment. I was holding a new driver, the one I just used. It has a very large white head. The pro approached and asked if I would like to try it out. I said sure, and he asked to see my swing. As I obliged, he was closely observing me and told me to lift my left shoulder during my backswing and try it again. The pro teed up a ball in front of the indoor net. He told me to take a few swings without hitting the ball.' I laughed and told him I already know how to do that. What I need to know is how to hit the ball!"

At the ladies tee, Dina got off a decent drive. Sandy gave Randy a dirty look and then a big smile. And then she hit a huge drive straight down the fairway.

Back in the cart, she continued to laugh and repeat, "Rat, rat, rat, rat! Look at that! All four balls within a few feet of each other."

Byron chose an eight iron, as did Randy. And both balls landed on the green.

Looking at the girls, Randy remarked, "You ladies should consider a seven iron."

"Not a chance," they replied in unison, and out came the eight irons.

Both balls, one after another, landed on the green. The girls did a little happy dance and gave the boys the finger. All four putts dropped into the cup.

Byron offered, "Let's do hole play, as I can see we are all good golfers. It will be more interesting than scoring."

"Okay," chimed Sandy, "it will be Randy and me against you two."

It was a beautiful sunny day in Florida with an azure blue sky. It was cloudless with just a light breeze. Hole after hole, they were even, and the game became very competitive.

As they rounded the turn to the tenth tee, Dina whispered to Sandy, "When you bend over to tee up the ball, maybe you should turn the other way. Your pink panties and shapely butt is definitely affecting Randy!"

"Ha! Maybe I'll do a little wiggle." Sandy thanked Dina with a wink.

The fairway shots from the eighteenth hole landed all four balls on the green. The score was still even. Sandy's ball was about ten feet uphill to the cup.

"Well, well. I guess us boys finally win! That's an impossible putt," Byron announced gleefully.

Waving her putter in the air, Sandy shouted, "Magic putter, do your thing!"

After taking a practice swing, she knocked the ball up the hill and into the cup. They all broke down laughing so loud that Adam and Vivian came over to see what was so funny.

"This was great fun!" exclaimed Randy. "Could we all have lunch together on the outdoor terrace?"

After a wonderful lunch, Randy pulled Sandy aside as everyone was leaving. "Sandy, can I see you this evening?"

"I am sorry, Randy. Tonight my father is the keynote speaker at the seminar dinner."

His disappointment showed. "How about tomorrow?"

"Oh, gosh. Tomorrow we have been invited to the home of a dear friend in Palm Beach Gardens, and then we are leaving for home early Sunday morning." But she smiled coyly. "Here is my home and cell numbers. I am going directly back to school and will have two weeks of hard studying for finals. But, Randy, please call me!"

As she looked at him directly, she couldn't help think, *Why doesn't he kiss me? I've given him so many opportunities.*

"I will call you, Sandy, and perhaps we can meet after finals."

Randy thought, *Why don't I have the courage to grab her and kiss her?*

After an awkward silence filled with words unsaid, they parted.

In the factory, standing by his golf cart, Randy asked, "Is everything ready? Then let's rock and roll. Turn on all the computers, all electrical switches, and all pumps. Fans on. Everyone in place!"

The Rand division of Carson Forester was in full production. After all the planning and all the preparation, Now was the moment. This complicated manufacturing process had never been tried before. The wall finish paint was so revolutionary that it could be a fantastic success or a complete failure.

The trailers were being loaded with deliveries. As one departed, another took its place. Randy, with Paula by his side, rode the golf cart back and forth from one end of the huge factory to the other, always checking, checking, checking. He was also worrying, trying to keep calm himself to keep the crew calm. The heating vats, the cooling pipes, and the intermixing of all the ingredients was progressing perfectly.

After two weeks of jubilation, Paula came to Randy's office. "We have an unusual problem. The reorders from the dealers are jamming the fax machine. The telephone is constantly ringing with calls from vendors begging me for more paint."

"Paula, I have been with the crew every day, and they are exhausted. The demand is taking its toll," Randy emphasized.

Paula continued, "Also we are low on money for payroll."

"Well, our dealers certainly know that payment is due in ten days after receiving an order," relayed Randy. "So we should be getting money from the Carson Forester finance office." Thinking for a few minutes, Randy said, "Paula, get me Jack Palmer on the phone."

After a few moments, he heard, "Good afternoon, Carson Forester's office. How may I direct your call?"

"Randy Forester for Jack Palmer, please."

After a couple minutes, Randy heard, "Hello, Randy. Jack Palmer here. How is everything?"

"Jack, I am calling to make sure that this coming Wednesday a money transfer will take place into my bank account."

There was silence on the other end.

"Jack? Jack? Are you there?"

"Randy, I'm going to lunch in a few minutes. I will call you from my cell phone."

A few minutes later, Randy's cell phone rang.

"Randy, I could get fired for this, so you have to promise to protect me if the crap hits the fan!"

"What are you talking about?" shouted Randy.

"I'm so sorry, Randy. Please don't get me fired! Mr. Peterson has directed me to hold up billing your orders. He told me he would notify me when to start sending out invoices. I want you to succeed, but I have to follow orders from Mr. Peterson."

With his mind spinning, Randy replied, "I appreciate the heads-up, Jack. When you return to the office, tell your secretary that I just wanted to say hello."

Turning to Paula, Randy said, "Please make arrangements for me to fly to Atlanta on Monday morning."

As he walked into Carson Forester headquarters Monday morning, he approached Mr. Peterson's secretary and announced himself, "Randy Forester to see Scott Peterson."

The secretary smiled. "Do you have an appointment? Mr. Peterson has given me strict instructions that he will not see anyone without an appointment."

"I do not have an appointment, but I will see Mr. Peterson now."

Maria let him enter.

Scott Peterson extended his hand in greeting. "It's good to see you, Randy."

"Scott, I will cut to the chase. I want you to advance one hundred thousand dollars immediately to be repaid by my funds and every ten days following until my funds catch up."

"Well, Randy, let me see if I can do that. I can only do it with authorization from your father."

Taking out his cell phone, Randy said, "Okay, Scott, I will call him now, and you can explain to him why you haven't sent out my invoices."

Scott put up his hand. "All right, that won't be necessary. I will transfer the money this afternoon."

"Thank you, Scott, and please remember to transfer the same amount to my bank account every Monday until the billing catches up."

"Listen up, everyone! It has become necessary to make some changes to the work shifts. Because of the volume of production, we know you are burnt out and exhausted. We will reduce each shift by two hours without a change in pay. Starting Monday, our shifts will be 9:00 a.m. to 3:00 p.m. and 3:00 p.m. to 9:00 p.m. Everyone will alternate shifts unless anyone wishes to remain on the 3:00 p.m. to 9:00 p.m. shift. This should help ease the burden. Paula, please speak with everyone and work it out. We cannot continue the eight-hour shifts. It is too tiring, and we cannot afford any errors."

"Hi, Mom! How are you and Dad?"

"Oh, Sandy, we are fine! How is the studying going?"

"I am doing well. I am almost ready for my exams. Mom, did Randy call?"

"No, honey, he has not called here. But you told me you gave him your number. You also told him that you were going to be very busy studying."

Sandy sighed. "He hasn't called me either. Do you think I should call him?"

"No, Sandy, I don't think you should call him. In my opinion, you should focus on school!"

"But Mom, I can't stop thinking about him. I really wish he would call!"

"Keep calm, sweetheart. I am sure he is busy."

"Hello, Mrs. Vanderbrook. This is Randy Forester. I've been calling your daughter on her cell phone, and she doesn't answer. Do you know where she is?"

"Oh, Randy! How nice to hear from you, dear! It just so happens that she is right here! Hold on."

"Randy!"

"Hi, Sandy! How are you? How is your studying going?"

"Why do you care?" Sandy replied defensively. "You've left me hanging for two weeks! You could have called, but you didn't. I thought about you every day!"

"Whoa, hold on a minute! You told me you were going to be very busy studying. I didn't want to disturb you! Listen, just because you are gorgeous and a big-time college graduate, that doesn't give you the right to beat me up! I really needed to talk to you, and I really need to see you." There was silence on the end of the line. "Sandy, are you there?"

"Yes, I am here, and I heard you loud and clear." Sandy couldn't contain her excitement as she gave her mother a big wink and smile.

The next hour was nonstop talking, joking, and telling graduation stories. Then the conversation turned serious as both of them were reluctant to hang up.

Randy blurted out, "I think I am falling in love with you!" He got flustered. "I really have to go. My day starts at 5:00 a.m. However, I have an invitation for you. Every year my grandparents have a weekend gathering of our family at their home. I told him I would bring a wonderful girl to the party to meet everyone. Please say yes!"

"Hold on, Randy. I'll need to ask my mother."

Mrs. Vanderbrook got on the phone. "Hello, Randy. This is a very concerned and protective mother. Do you promise to take very good care of her?"

"Of course, Mrs. Vanderbrook, I do promise, and I take my responsibilities very seriously."

Mrs. Vanderbrook put Sandy back on the phone.

"Randy, I would be honored to meet your family, but first …" She motioned to her mother to pick up the phone extension. "I really want to hear again those very exciting words that you said to me."

"I think I have fallen in love with you!"

Sandy could hardly catch her breath. "I think the same." She choked back a sob.

Randy felt weak in the knees. "My assistant Paula will be in touch with you in the morning to make arrangements. Good night!"

As they hung up the phone, Sandy and her mother burst into tears of joy.

———◆———

"Good morning. May I speak with Miss Vanderbrook, please?"

"Speaking," Sandy replied.

"My name is Paula. I am Randy's assistant. If it is satisfactory, Sam will pick you up on Saturday morning at nine thirty. He will take you to the airport, where you will board Randy's jet to Atlanta. The family is staying at the Willard Hotel. I have reserved a room for you for Saturday night. Randy will meet you there. He has a suite permanently reserved, as his grandfather owns the hotel. He makes frequent trips to Atlanta, where his company is headquartered. I hope this is satisfactory?"

"Yes, thank you, Paula! Can you spare a few minutes for girl talk?"

"Yes, of course!"

"How should I dress?"

"You will need two outfits: one for Saturday night and one for Sunday night. Neat and casual. Not too sexy! I heard about your golf outfit! They are really great people, very down to earth. Just be yourself."

"Thank you, Paula. I hope I will have the opportunity to meet you."

"If you want to endear yourself and see something spectacular, ask him for a tour of our factory. Then you will see over sixty employees and myself all in love with our Randy. But don't worry. I am engaged to a wonderful man, and besides, I am too old for him!"

Both ladies giggled and said good-bye.

Chapter 4

In front of the hotel, her shapely legs with black patent leather high heels emerged from the limo. Waving to Randy, who was waiting at the curb, she stepped out. A startled Randy, totally in awe of her beauty, just stood and stared. Sandy ran to him and put her arms around his neck. She then drew him toward her body, and they kissed with the emotion of their first kiss. Randy's knees turned to rubber as all of the bystanders cheered and applauded. They separated and walked into the hotel, hand in hand.

In her hotel room, they embraced again as they heard a knock at the door. It was Randy's mother.

"Hello, Sandy." She extended her hand in greeting. "I am so glad you could join us. The limo is picking us all up in thirty minutes. Sandy, I suggest you change into something more casual."

As they all gathered in the lobby, Sandy emerged from the elevator as everyone turned to greet her. "Hello, everyone. Thank you for including me in your family."

At the entrance of the spacious screened-in patio, Carson and his wife Eleanor stood greeting everyone, hugging, kissing, and being genuinely happy to be together.

"Grandma, Grandpa, thank you for inviting me. I am honored."

Grandma took her hand and welcomed her warmly. Then Grandpa gave a big hug.

"We are delighted to meet you. Randy calls us several times each weekend, and all he talks about is you. I beg you, Sandy, to take your actions seriously, as he is hopelessly in love with you."

Returning his hug, she replied, "I will, Grandpa. I will."

As the laughter, the storytelling, the family anecdotes, the good-natured ribbing, and the never-ending delicious buffet began to wrap up, finally Carson announced, "This Sunday, brunch will start at one in the dining room. Good night, everyone."

Sandy was reeling with emotion when she was with this great family.

Walking to her hotel room together, Randy stood at the doorway.

She grabbed his shirt, pulled him into the room, and whispered, "You are going to make love to me now."

She pushed him down on the edge of the bed and stood in front of him. Slowly teasing, she undressed. When completely naked, she pressed against him and brushed his cheeks with her breasts. "Now it's your turn."

He quickly undressed but had difficulty removing his shorts because of his rock-hard erection. Sandy reached down and gently held it in her hands. She climbed on the bed, and he followed swiftly. He leaned on his elbows and gave a deep, tender kiss with all of the love he had. He then gently kissed her cheek and then her neck and briefly touched her taut nipples with his tongue. He turned her over. He relished in the moment as he fondled her back and buttocks.

She then rolled back over. "I can't wait another second." She stretched out her arms to him and swiftly slipped on a condom.

The two were in another world as they rocked back and forth in unison.

After Sunday brunch was over, Carson stood and clinked his glass. "Please give me your undivided attention, please. As chairman of the board of directors for our company, this business portion of our meeting is now open for serious conversation. Considering we as a family are the sole owners, we have much to discuss. But before we begin, I wish to welcome Sandra Vanderbrook. I want you all to know that she has recently graduated from George Washington University with honors and will now enter the George Washington Law School. Sandy, we are very pleased to welcome you!"

Sandy stood with complete self-assurance. "Thank you, everyone, for your warm welcome. I am deeply honored to be invited. Grandpa, if you have any influence with your grandson, please urge him to ask for my hand in marriage." Amid the shouting and applause, she sat down, smiling broadly.

Carson resumed, "I will now turn over the discussion to Adam."

"Thank you, Dad. We had an excellent year. Sales are up to 28 percent, and our profits are exceeding expectations. Our new advertising campaign will begin in two weeks. We have added over twelve hundred new dealers and are expanding rapidly. Our new plant in Ontario is at full capacity. Now we will ask Randy for his report on our newest division. As you leave, please pick up your very generous bonus check."

"Thank you, Dad. Before I start my report, I would like to make a statement to my love, Sandy. In my wildest dreams,

I could never imagine to be so fortunate to be loved by a girl so smart and so beautiful." As he looked at her, he realized she was overcome with emotion being with this great family.

Randy continued, "The Rand division is also wildly successful. MajDec is a fantastic product, and the demand for it by decorators, contractors, and consumers alike has far exceeded expectations. We have produced and sold over five million color decks. We have mastered a manufacturing process that is very unique. If the demand stays strong for another six months, I believe we will know if this is a stable product or if the market will be saturated. The Rand division presently has a million dollars in the bank; however, we have not repaid the initial investment. Now I have several requests for your consideration. I would like your approval to hire Tom Bailey as plant manager. I am asking approval to transfer the financial department to be under my control in my plant. I am asking to do my own financial and accounting office."

The vote was unanimous in favor.

As they walked to the limo holding hands, he said, "Sandy, I know you are bursting to know the amount of my bonuses."

"Only if you want me to know," she replied.

"Okay, but what is the reward?"

"Well, you can kiss me."

"Where?"

"Anywhere you would like to."

He showed her a two hundred and fifty thousand-dollar check. She wrapped his neck with her arms and drew him to her, and they shared a long kiss.

"That's going to have to hold you for now," she whispered.

"Sandy, regarding the other matter that you brought up at the meeting, it is only proper for me to speak to you parents first."

"Okay, lover, it's your move."

———◆———

"Paula, please get me Tom Bailey on the phone."

After a few moments, Randy said, "Hello, Tom. I am calling to offer you the job of Rand division plant manager. I want you to know that it is a very demanding technical job, if you are interested. I can have Sam pick you up tomorrow morning, and we can have lunch and discuss it."

"Randy, that would be great. Thank you for the opportunity," replied Tom.

"No thanks needed. We are a family with a family business."

Randy hung up and said, "Paula, make all arrangements to pick up my cousin, Tom Bailey, tomorrow morning. Also I want you to join for the tour of the plant and lunch as I offered him the job of plant manager."

The next morning, Randy remarked, "Tom, this is not an easy position. We do a very technical high manufacturing process. There is no room for errors. Everyone working here is a very dedicated professional. If you agree, Paula will brief you on the equipment and all the intricate details. Your salary will be two thousand dollars a week. What do you say? Are you ready for a wild ride?"

"Absolutely," replied Tom. "When do I start?"

"Great. Have Sam help you find temporary accommodations. You start tomorrow morning at six thirty."

Randy then hung up and called out, "Paula, get me Jack Palmer on the phone."

Jack's voicemail picked up, and Randy said, "Hello, Jack. When you go out for lunch, call me."

Ten minutes later, Randy heard, "Randy, Jack Palmer on the phone for you."

Randy then said, "Hello, Jack. I am bringing all of my financial and accounting here to Jacksonville. I need to have full control. I am offering you the position of chief financial officer. You will be in complete control of everyday building, furnishing, hiring, and setting up a complete finance department. It is an enormous responsibility, but I know you are very capable. I want you to know first that we are only in business seven months. You will have to move with your family to Jacksonville. If you are interested, take Wednesday off. Sam will pick you up, and we will discuss this over lunch. Please let me know by the end of the day tomorrow, okay?"

Randy then hung up and called out, "Paula, please find Mrs. Jack Palmer, and arrange a phone call."

Paula then said momentarily, "Randy, Mrs. Palmer on the phone."

Randy immediately began talking, "Hello, Mrs. Palmer. I am calling to discuss the job offer with your husband."

"I already know, Mr. Forester. He called me."

"Mrs. Palmer, would you agree to accompany Jack on Wednesday when we discuss this offer? I would appreciate the opportunity of discussing this with you both. Please have Jack confirm that you will join us."

Randy heard Paula say, "Randy, Scott Peterson calling for you. What shall I tell him?"

"Paula, here is exactly what you tell him, not one word more and, if necessary, repeat it. Mr. Forester is too busy to speak with you."

"Randy, I've made all arrangements to pick up Mr. and Mrs. Palmer on Wednesday."

"Great, Paula. I want you to join us."

Sandy arrived home very late Sunday night and went directly to her bedroom. On Monday evening at dinner, she related every detail to her parents: how they greeted her, what they said in every conversation, and who everyone present was. She talked about the business details on Sunday. She told them everything that had transpired, and her parents were thrilled. The only part she left out was the sex she had with Randy. She later described it to her mother while they were in the kitchen.

"Good morning, Randy. Reza Sanchez wishes to speak to you."

"Hi, Reza. What's up?"

"Randy, we have something to discuss. When can you be in Boca?"

"I'll see you Thursday morning, Reza."

"That's perfect, Randy. Meet me in the lab."

At lunch with Jack Palmer, his wife, and Paula, Randy said, "I appreciate you making the trip here. I realize this is a big decision. I also believe this is a great opportunity for you. I know you are very capable of this responsibility. I need to have full control of my own finances. My plan is to have three managers. Tom Bailey, my cousin, is a plant manager. If you accept, you will be finance manager. Paula, I'm appointing you as operations manager. You three will assist in making this division a success. Each of you will start at two thousand a week."

After a series of questions and answers, an hour later, Randy stood. "Why don't you have Sam show you some of the residential area and also check out the schools? Jack, I'll need an answer by the end of the day on Friday."

"Good morning, everyone. Reza, Arnold, Norman, how are you feeling? How are you enjoying your new income?" asked Randy.

Norman, sitting in his favorite lounge chair, asked, "Arnold, would you please fill in Randy on our new development? How about some coffee, Randy?"

"No thanks. I'm excited to hear Arnold's presentation."

Arnold responded, "First the two scientists you pay to help us are excellent, but we are finished with that phase. Second, as you know, Norman was hospitalized with pneumonia. While there, his mind was always searching. We are presently testing a wall paint that will have several types of antibiotics added to the base. It will only be available in an off white, and as we progress the process, it becomes very technical. It's not easy to find the correct methods or equipment to continue testing. However, if we are successful, the market could be limitless. Imagine if hospitals, clinics, and more would coat the walls with this product. It will eliminate infections and viruses. We would like you to continue the services of the two scientists that you pay to help us with the intricate testing. Our main problem is how long it will be effective and whether it can be manufactured at a cost that would be acceptable. If we can perfect the formulas and invent this product, would you be interested?"

Randy was thoughtful. "I am definitely interested, but first it would have to be sold under the Carson Forester label. That means we guarantee it. Second, can it be sold at the price that would warrant the cost of producing it? Third, could it be marketed directly to the end user and not through our dealers? Finally, how much would it cost to outfit the needed equipment, and how large of an area would it take? When you tell me it's ready and we can successfully patent it, I believe the worldwide demand would be very vast."

"Hello, Mom. How are you? I am calling to tell you that I plan to propose to Sandy. I'm not sure when because I am extremely busy, but most likely this weekend."

"That's wonderful, Randy! Keep me updated, please!"

"Hello, Mrs. Vanderbrook. This is Randy. I have to talk to you and Dr. Vanderbrook."

"Randy, is it about you and Sandy?"

"Yes, I need your permission to propose to her."

"Randy, that would be wonderful! We'd love to have you as a part of our family."

"Hello, Mom. It's me again. I need to buy an engagement ring, but I don't know anything about rings! However, you certainly do. Could you help me out?"

"Absolutely! I would like to call Sandy's mother. Perhaps she would meet me at the 47th Street Jewelry Exchange in Manhattan. But Randy, to buy an outstanding diamond ring, you have to consider spending about twenty-five to thirty thousand dollars."

"Mom, that would be great. Have it delivered to me, and I will give you a certified bank check in payment."

"Hi, Sandy. What are you doing this Saturday evening?"

She laughed. "Why? Are you asking me for a date? I know you spoke with my mother, but she would not tell me anything, and I have not had a night's sleep since. So please come early."

Randy arrived at the Vanderbrook home Saturday afternoon. A raucous shouting erupted. He saw Sandy's parents, Byron and Dina, and his own Aunt Vanessa and Uncle Franklin.

For a moment, Randy was startled and shouted, "Is this fabulous or what!"

Randy's mother laughed. "There is no way you are going to propose without us all being present."

As they all hugged and kissed, Sandy walked into the room.

"Dearest Sandy, you know I love you." He took her hand and slipped the ring on her finger. "Please grant me the greatest honor. Will you marry me?"

She threw her arms around his neck as she looked at the ring and whispered, "Yes, yes! And what a magnificent ring!"

Vanessa sat down at her grand piano and started to play and sing a wonderful love song, "Be My Love and End This Yearning." Everyone joined in singing and wiping away tears of joy.

———◆———

"Good morning, Randy. Jack Palmer has accepted your offer. He will give his company two weeks' notice," said Paula. "Also I have hired a moving company for them and recommended a real estate broker. I also told Mr. Palmer that we would be paying all costs."

"Excellent, Paula. I am very busy today. Coordinate the new schedule changes, and when you have all the employee changes completed, catch up with Tom and me."

Arriving at the plant early Monday morning, Randy was surprised to see Jack Palmer in deep conversation with Paula.

"What happened, Jack?"

"Well, as I informed Paula, Scott Peterson fired me immediately. Paula reserved a hotel room for me, and Sam picked me up this morning."

"That's great news, Jack. We are glad you are here."

Very early the next morning, Randy and Tom were working on a plan to possibly increase production when Paula called.

"Randy, could you return to your office?"

"Sure, but I need about fifteen more minutes with Tom, and I will be there."

As he approached his office, while driving his golf cart, he almost drove into the wall. There waiting for him was Sandy. She was wearing tight jeans and a Jaguar baseball jersey and cap. They kissed and hugged each other in a tight embrace.

"Paula, why didn't you tell me it was Sandy?"

Sandy chimed in, "She sent Sam to pick me up, and I asked her to keep it a surprise." She gave Paula a wink as she left the office. "Honey, I wanted to see for myself what you have created here, and I want a complete tour."

Taking her hand but still in shock, Randy said, "Okay, hop in the golf cart. The tour is about to begin."

Driving slowly along the assembly lines, he held her hand and described what was happening at each station.

"Bill, have you seen Tom?"

"Yes, Randy, he is behind vat number two, checking the heating gauges."

"Thanks."

"Tom, where are you?" he called out. "Can you come here for a minute?"

Coming from behind the large vat, Tom asked, "What is it, Randy?"

When he saw Sandy, he pulled off his overalls and gloves and hugged her. "What a beautiful guest!"

"Listen, Tom. We are going to have dinner tonight at the Primrose Café on the outdoor terrace. If you are free, will you join us?"

"I would love to," replied Tom. "Can I bring my girlfriend?"

"You're so sly. I didn't know you even had a girlfriend. I'll make reservations for four at seven thirty. It's casual."

"Randy honey, I haven't checked into a hotel yet. My overnight bag is still in the car."

"Don't fret. Knowing Sam, I can assure you that your bag isn't in the car. It's waiting for you in the room already."

A little later, Randy announced, "Paula, I'm leaving."

"Does Paula lock up?" asked Sandy.

"No, we're working late shifts and have twenty-four-hour security inside and out."

"Hi, Sam. Thanks a lot for not giving me a signal," said Randy.

They all laughed.

Chapter 5

Entering the lobby of the beautiful Willard Hotel, Randy heard, "Good afternoon, Mr. Forester."

"Hello, Bob. Say hello to Sandy."

"My pleasure, ma'am. Sam brought your luggage into room 2602. Here are the entry cards."

"Honey, how did he know?"

"Well, my father and I own the hotel. Grandpa Carson deeded it to us."

"Oh!"

"My permanent suite is next door, room 2601."

Stepping into the room and closing the door, Sandy was already taking off her clothes and standing before him completely naked. He was staring in complete awe at her beauty. She laughed and helped him remove his clothes as he was somewhat in a trance. His entire body began to tremble with anticipation as she pulled him onto the bed. Taking his erection in her hand, she slipped on a condom and directed it toward her. As they rocked back and forth, their intense love was magical. The world did not exist as they exploded in each other's arms.

As they were standing together in the shower, not a word was spoken as they attempted to return to earth.

The phone rang. "Mr. Forester, your car is waiting, sir."

"Thanks, Bob."

"Good evening, Mr. Forester. Welcome to Primrose. Your party is already here. I seated them in the garden, as you asked."

"Thank you, Maria."

Every table was occupied as they walked into the garden. Sandy suddenly let go of his hand and dashed to a table in the corner calling, "Joann! Joann!"

The girl sitting there jumped up. "Sandy! Sandy!"

They hugged. Tom and Randy looked at each other, perplexed.

Tom spoke first, "What is going on here? Are we missing something between you two?"

"No," replied Sandy. "Randy, please say hello to Joann Wallace. We were together for two years at George Washington University. We had almost all the same classes. We graduated together as a matter a fact at the graduation procession, and we stood together, V and W. Many nights we studied together and ate Chinese takeout."

Joann demurely gave Randy a slight kiss on the cheek and continued, "Tom and I met at a George Washington fraternity party. A good friend, a student member of the fraternity, invited him. Tom was at Wharton. His friend was at George Washington."

"This is unbelievable!"

They both shouted and hugged again. And for the next two hours, they ate, drank, and told college stories.

Tom spoke as calmly as possible, "We have to leave. I have a big day tomorrow and have to be at the plant very early to meet the city inspectors."

"Joann, what are your plans?" asked Sandy.

"I am entering George Washington Law School in two weeks."

"So am I," replied Sandy.

"Have you made dormitory arrangements?"

"No, have you?"

"No, I am trying to find an apartment, as I find it difficult to study in a dorm."

Randy held up his hand. "Would you both consider an apartment together?"

"Randy, what kind of trick do you have up your sleeve?" asked Sandy.

"My father and I happen to own a residential hotel not far from George Washington. They are beautiful two-bedroom, two-bathroom apartments. You two could select whatever furniture you wanted, and when you graduate, I will have a furnished unit. Think it over, and let me know."

Approaching the twenty-sixth floor at the hotel, Randy asked, "Would you come up to my suite for a nightcap?"

She took his hand. "Only if I can stay for breakfast."

Once in the room, they fell into bed in each other's arms.

Sandy whispered, "Don't hold me so tight. I will not try to escape."

At seven the next morning, Randy was sitting in a large chair, staring at Sandy. He marveled at how her blonde hair spread over her pillow with wondrous beauty.

She stirred and opened her eyes. "You're staring at me again. You make me nervous."

"Sandy, I cannot believe the most wonderful girl is sleeping in my bed."

"Never mind the sweet talk. Where is my breakfast?"

"Sandy, I had plans to see my dad at company headquarters today. Would you come with me?"

"I would love to accept. But I have to be home for a Saturday morning tennis match."

"A tennis match!" he exclaimed.

"Yes, Byron and I are in the semifinals of the statewide country club tennis tournament. Also I forgot to tell you. Since we have a family membership, I added your name as a family member."

"That's interesting. I did not know that you are such a hotshot tennis player."

"We can have Sam take us to Atlanta and see Dad. Then I will take you home and return here, okay?"

Picking up the phone, Randy said, "Good morning, Paula. Please ask Sam to pick us up in one hour and have the jet ready. Also Paula, please arrange a meeting Monday with Tom, Jack, you, and me. We will be flying to Atlanta to see my father. Then we will take Sandy home to New Jersey, and then Sam will bring us back."

"Hi, Dad. I am a little late because I brought Sandy with me."

Adam came over, and he and Sandy hugged.

"It's great to see you, Sandy. Is my son treating you right?"

"Yes, sir."

And they both laughed.

"Dad, here is the situation. Jack Palmer is now my CFO. I want the entire financial department under my control. Cousin Tom would be plant manager. We are presently shipping daily, approximately forty thousand gallons. However, our backlog of orders is growing every day. Our dealers are pleading for more. The demand for MajDec is strong."

"The reason we cannot meet the demand is twofold. One is that we are not receiving enough of the bases we need from the Dallas plant. As many times as I ask why, I have no real answer. We only use one product in three bases. It should be easy to increase production. Two is that shipping from Dallas to Jacksonville is unreliable and costly, which reduces our profit margin. Would it be possible to give me the other half of my plant? Then I can manufacture the bases in the quantities I need and then pump it directly into the vats."

"That's sounds like a good plan," replied Adam. "However, I will order a complete study and confer with Dallas managers and also Jacksonville to see if it can be done. I will bring it up at the next meeting, and I will need you to be present to answer any questions." Finally, Adam said, "Randy, I know how hard you are working and dedicated to succeed, but try not to irritate too many company officials, okay?"

"Yes, Dad. Now one more item of interest. The Boca group is testing a new product. It is too early to tell if it will work, and I am underwriting some of the testing costs. It is a white-only wall paint that, if it can be successfully blended with many different antibiotics, it will eliminate the infectious viruses that have plagued hospitals and clinics. But as for now, it is only in the testing stage."

"Sounds interesting, Randy. It could be a perfect first for your division."

"If it can be proven, this is something we should consider. Let's talk about more important things. If there is anything new that you two are planning, please keep us informed."

Turning to Sandy, Adam asked, "How is your wonderful family? We are still rehashing the excitement over the engagement. I know the two mothers are in almost daily contact and have become good friends, and they are completely absorbed in wedding plans."

"I am really happy that our families will be united," replied Sandy, "and grow to be one."

"That's wonderful, Sandy dear. Just keep us doting parents informed."

———◆———

"Hi, Randy sweetheart. What are you doing?"

"Hi to you also, Sandy. I just got home, and I am relaxing in my favorite lounge chair with a Grey Goose on ice. In my mind, I am picturing your smile and laughter. How about you?"

"If you were paying attention, which you weren't," said Sandy, "you would recall that Byron and I are in semifinals of the minor club tennis tournament last Saturday. We won, so this Sunday we play at North Jersey Club for the trophy, which is a very big deal here. The problem is that Byron cannot be my partner as he could not refuse to do emergency surgery on some big-time athlete. It is very intricate and requires he operate personally. So I need a partner, or else we forfeit and I leave the country, never to return. Since I added your name to our family membership, you qualify."

"I can do it."

"Randy, seriously? Have you ever played any tennis?"

"Yes, I played a little in college. If I agree, is there a reward?" replied Randy.

"You rat! A reward?" Sandy shouted. "I very willingly give you my body. You don't need any money. What else is there?"

"Sandy, you could talk to me about setting a date. I'm worried you might meet someone else in law school."

"Randy honey, that will never happen." She continued, "Also the following Wednesday, Joann and I are flying to DC to register for our classes."

"Sandy, there is no chance that you are standing in line at the airport and flying a commercial jet. No Forester will fly anything but a private plane. Do you understand?"

"Yes, master!"

"Call Paula, and tell her your plans. She will arrange everything, including the apartment. Also I will be happy to be your partner in the tennis tournament so we can lose gracefully. However, I will not arrive until late Saturday night, as we are installing some new equipment. Please reserve a hotel room for me, and tell Paula the details. I will be ready to do battle on Sunday, but I will have to return here Sunday evening to be ready for Monday with new equipment in place, okay?"

"Paula, please get me Bob Fellows of Fellows, Smith, and Jones on the phone."

After a few moments, Randy heard, "Good morning. You have reached the law offices of Fellows, Smith, and Jones."

"Thank you. Randy Forester wishes to speak with Mr. Fellows."

Randy then heard Mr. Fellows pick up the line. "Hello, Bob. I need you to file an application for a zoning change and schedule an inspection for Friday, as we are starting production on Monday in our new facilities."

"Randy, would it be all right if I have one of the other partners handle this, as I wanted to leave early on Friday? As you are a golfer, perhaps you would understand. My son has invited me to be his partner at a member guest outing at his club on Sunday. The Oaks in Rumson, New Jersey, where he lives with his family. Also my wife is looking forward to seeing him play. Please, I am asking you to allow one of my partners to handle this for you."

"Bob, this is a coincidence. I am flying to Rumson on Saturday to play in a tennis tournament with my fiancée, Sandy Vanderbrook, and I'm returning on Sunday night. If you would agree, I could pick you and your wife up, along with anyone else that wishes to join us. We would fly early Saturday morning to New Jersey and return Sunday evening in my private jet."

"Many thanks, Randy. That will work out just fine."

"Good. Paula will call you to make all arrangements, Bob. I really appreciate you doing this for me."

———❖———

On Sunday morning, as Sandy waited in the lobby of the hotel, she saw several photographers standing near the elevators. She overheard one say, "The desk clerk called me to report that Randolph Forester checked in last night. We are hoping to find out why."

As Randy emerged, the questions began. "What are you doing here, Mr. Forester? What's in the bag? Is that a tennis racquet in there?"

"I am meeting my true love, Sandra Vanderbrook. We are in a tennis tournament."

Once he spied Sandy, he rushed over to her. They kissed and hugged, oblivious to the public and the photographers. They left the locker room holding hands and looking around to determine if anyone noticed they had been there for a while. Sandy looked beautiful in a pale pink short skirt with white underpants, a white sleeveless top with pink stripes, and matching sneakers. Randy looked quite sporty in a University of Pennsylvania sweatshirt and matching shorts with his oldest, scruffy-looking sneakers and no socks.

A tall, young man and an equally tall young woman were waiting for them.

"I am Nels, and this is Eldra. We're the ones that will kick your asses today. I watched you both play last week. I could see that you didn't win. Actually the other team lost." It was obvious that they didn't realize that Sandy had a different partner today.

Randy pressed Sandy's hand, and she understood his reason that they should not swallow the bait.

Nels, smiling at Eldra, continued, "Can you believe that these two kids think they can beat us? What a joke." He continued with a smirk, "Not that it makes any difference, but we didn't get your names."

"This is Sandy, and I am Randy."

Eldra laughed. "You sound like a vaudeville team. Do you also sing and dance? I hope you can handle the embarrassment of a huge defeat in front of your members because we're going to show you a real dance."

Randy, still holding hands, turned and whispered, "Don't take the bait. It's a very old trick."

As they walked away, Nels called out, "How about a wager to make it more interesting?"

Randy turned around. "I don't bet. It makes me nervous."

Nels snickered and called out, "How about five hundred dollars?"

There was no response from Randy.

"How about a thousand?" He turned to Eldra to say, "Too bad. We could have made a quick thousand."

Walking onto the court, Sandy spied her parents in the bleachers and blew them a kiss.

Randy waved and opened his bag. "Sandy, I have a present for you." He took out a brand-new tennis racquet.

She looked at it and gasped. "A Vermeer racquet? My gosh! The pro was just showing me pictures of this new amazing racquet. As I recall, it was very expensive." She took a few swings. "This is fantastic!"

Randy signaled the judge. "Could we please have a few volleys to become familiar with the surface of the court floor?"

The judge nodded approval. After they had lobbed a few times, he signaled the judge that they were ready. Eldra won the toss, so she would serve first.

Randy whispered, "Let them win the first set, okay?"

The serve was perfect. Sandy returned it, and Eldra returned it to her. Sandy ran for it but missed. Bounce. Bounce. Nels served. Fault. The second serve was perfect, low over the net to Randy. He let it out of bounds. Nels and Eldra high-fived. As they volleyed back and forth, Randy missed the next serve and the following.

"First set to Nutley Country Club."

Randy stood at the line and pointed to the ball boy, who threw him a ball. He pointed again with two fingers extended. The ball boy threw him two more. Randy fingered, then selected one, put the other in his pocket, bounced a few times, threw the ball ten feet high, and came down with a powerful serve that was lightning fast. Nels never even saw it coming. On the next serve, Randy aimed directly at Nels. The ball hit him in the stomach so hard that he fell backward. Randy gave him a weak, "Sorry."

Sandy's serve was textbook, low over the net. Her serve was returned. Sandy sent it back into the corner in bounds. The next serve was to Randy. He gave the ball a crushing sideswipe. It spun wildly over the net and fell to the ground.

Sandy looked at him, laughing. "I played a little tennis in college. Oh, I played a little golf in college," she said, mimicking him, "and I see you have a Vermeer racquet. Don't tell me. A gift from your grandfather?"

"Actually it was from my mother, but close enough."

The serves were perfect, but Randy's spinning returns were impossible.

"Second set to Rumson."

"Third set to Rumson."

Nels and Eldra were on the verge of tears due to utter frustration.

"Sandy, it's your serve. Throw the ball higher, and with all your strength, try to kill it."

It was evident that Nels and Eldra were at the verge of collapse. Nels signaled to the judge and, in a low voice, conceded the match.

"Sandy, I have to leave immediately."

He waved to her parents. They kissed and hugged. He left without changing his clothes. At the banquet that night, where the trophy was awarded, brother and sister accepted amid loud applause.

A few hours later, Randy called Sandy. "Hi, Sandy. I just arrived home. I apologize for leaving in such a hurry. How was the award ceremony?"

"It was wonderful. Our friends and the members can't stop talking about your game! You are a star! Tomorrow Joann and I will be leaving for DC. I will call you when we're settled, okay?"

A few days later, she called again. "Hi, Randy. Don't come to DC this weekend, as we are in over our heads with schedules and details. I love you. Talk to you soon."

——◆——

The following Thursday, Paula said, "Reza is on the phone for you, Randy."

Randy picked up. "Good morning, Reza. How is the testing process progressing?"

"That's why I'm calling you, Randy. Our testing is almost complete, and the product looks magnificent. We are waiting to hear from you as to whether you are interested or not. We cannot give you cost figures because I'm sure you're in a better position to purchase the five antibiotics that are needed to complete the formula. Several factors are in this process. It's only available in white, and the base paint is the same as your base number one. We have not applied for a patent yet. We will not go any further depending on your possible involvement."

"Reza, I cannot make a commitment without more information. Please send all the paperwork and samples, six drawdowns, six quart samples of the finished product, and a list of the five crucial antibiotics needed. I will hire a cost accounting firm and have them sign a secrecy agreement. If satisfactory, I will ask you to accompany me to Atlanta to make a presentation when everything is completed, okay?"

"Thank you, Randy. Everything will be ready for Sam tomorrow morning."

He hung up and called his cousin. "Where are you, Tom?"

"Hi. What are you doing this weekend? Sandy called and said not to meet them in DC yet, as they are too busy."

"Randy, I think I'll go home. I haven't seen my parents in a while. Also my sister Alexis flew home from England for a few days. It's some sort of holiday at Oxford University."

"That's great, Tom. Actually I haven't seen Alexis either in more than a year."

"Well, no one has, but she will be graduating this fall."

"That's a good idea. I'll call my mother and see what plans they have made."

Randy then called his parents, and his dad picked up. "Randy, this is your father. I just heard the good news! You are coming home this weekend. Please stop by my office early Friday afternoon."

"I'll swing by at around two. See you then, Pops. I love you."

➤◇➥

As Randy walked into the executive suite, all the staff surrounded him and warmly greeted him.

"Hi, Dad. How are the new golf clubs? Is Mom still beating you? You don't have to answer."

Adam laughed as they hugged. "Let's get to the report because I want you to come with me. I am purchasing a new set of woods that are being custom-fitted. I promised Mom that we wouldn't be delayed, as she's anxious to see you. I'm glad to hear that Tom is working out so fantastically."

"Tom really is a gem, Dad. He's taken over managing the plant and has proven to be naturally brilliant at the extremely technical procedure. He has made improvements that even the engineers were amazed with. Jack Palmer is a natural leader. I made the right decision. My finance office is operating smoothly and efficiently. His expertise and advice is outstanding. The move to manufacture my own bases is a winner. We now pump the paint directly into the vats. We are in control and have increased our profit by not having to unload drums, lift them to the second floor, open them, and pour the paint into the vats. We now have no backlogs of orders. Dad, our global market is just opening up, so now we can deliver."

"MajDec has taken the decorating world by storm. How long the popularity will last? No one knows. Now the group that invented MajDec has come up with a new product that has been offered to us. It's a wall coating that is combined by a very intricate process with antibiotics. When coated on the walls of hospitals, clinics, and other medical facilities, it will eliminate all infections and viruses effectively for at least two years. I have hired a consultant to investigate the costs. The market could be huge, but the cost to manufacture could be very high. I will keep you informed because, if you approve a study, we would need larger facilities and more employees."

The following Thursday afternoon, Randy drove his golf cart the length of the plant.

"Hi, Tom. I'm looking for you. What are your thoughts regarding the phone call we received last night telling us to cancel our flight to DC for the weekend?"

"Well, Randy, I guess we have to rely on what we are told. The workload in law school is more than expected, and they need the weekend to study and complete the assignments."

"I hope you're right, Tom, because I'm not very happy about this. In fact, I just decided that I'm going to the Breakers Hotel in Palm Beach to play a few rounds of golf to calm me down. I was hoping that you could join me."

"That sounds great, Randy. Just like old times."

"Okay, Tom. I'll pick you up tomorrow at your apartment at about three. We can be there in time for a relaxing dinner and a few drinks. I'll have Paula reserve a two-bedroom suite and make all the necessary tee times. We'll use the chopper so we can land on hotel grounds."

Chapter 6

E ntering the hotel lobby, Randy heard, "Good afternoon, Mr. Forester. It's a pleasure to see you again."

"Hello, Bob. This is my cousin, Thomas Bailey."

"Pleasure to meet you. Your suite is ready, gentlemen, and your luggage is on the way. Your golf bags were picked up and will be waiting for you in your cart. You have a 10:00 a.m. tee time."

"Thank you, Bob."

They were both rather exhausted and unanimously decided to have room service deliver dinner. By nine thirty, they were both sound asleep.

"I don't know about you, Randy, but after nine hours of sleep, I'm ready to go to war."

"Me too, Tom. I don't know about you, but this is just what I needed."

The day was glorious. The sun shined bright, and the sky glowed a perfect blue.

The starter approached them and asked very politely, "Gentlemen, I have a very nice couple ready to tee off. Would you consider joining them?"

Standing at the tee was a very distinguished middle-aged man and an attractive lady. They waved.

"Sure, that would be fine."

"Good morning. I'm Randy, and this is my cousin Tom."

The man replied, "We are pleased you are joining us. I'm John, and this is my lovely wife Anita. Why don't we tee off and then drive to the ladies tee?"

John teed up his ball, gave his driver a few swings, and sent the ball straight down the fairway out of sight.

"What a great drive!" exclaimed both Tom and Randy in unison.

Randy's drive was a powerful shot, both long and straight. It was followed by Tom's robust drive. At the ladies tee, Anita teed up, took a few practice swings, and sent the ball soaring down the fairway.

As they drove down the fairway, Tom broke the silence, "I know that man from somewhere. I just can't place him."

Everyone had a par. As the game progressed, the score continued to be even, and it became a rather exciting match. At the ninth tee, the score was still even.

Suddenly Tom blurted out, "It took me a while, but now I recognize you, sir. You're the United States Senate Majority Leader! John Attersby of Georgia, if I recall correctly?"

"Why yes, that is me. But please respect our wishes for privacy, as we just wanted a tranquil weekend of golf."

"Absolutely, Mr. Attersby. My name is Randolph Forester, and this is my cousin, Thomas Bailey. His father Franklin is an attorney and well known in the Atlanta area."

"Oh yes! I have met him and Vanessa at many functions, and of course I'm a great admirer of your grandfather, Carson." He paused. "Now let me see who's going to win this match."

After a spirited back nine, the score ended up even. They shook hands around and remarked about the most enjoyable round.

"Fellows, if you ever need anything in DC, just call me. Thanks for a great game. It was wonderful meeting the both of you."

They drove away contently.

"How do we top this great day so far?"

"Paula made dinner reservations for us at seven thirty at the Green Tequila in Palm Beach. Knowing Paula, she made a good choice."

The maître d' greeted them at the restaurant, "May I be of service?"

"Yes, a reservation for two under the name of Paula."

"Ah, yes. If you gentlemen would follow me, I have strict instructions on where to seat you."

They were seated in a booth against the center wall in the middle of all of the action.

Tom remarked, "That Paula is a gem. This is way better than a Broadway show. Will you look at all these beautiful people?"

"I really am glad we decided to wear summer slacks and sports jackets."

A young man wearing a tuxedo approached. "May I get you gentlemen something to drink?"

"Absolutely," they both replied. "What's the specialty of the house?"

"Why, green tequila of course! Is that okay?"

In no more than three minutes, they were both sipping their green tequilas, and Randy remarked, "This place is fantastic, but there is a slight sexual awareness in the air."

"You're a 100 percent right," replied Tom, signaling the server they were ready to order dinner.

Out of the corner of his eye, Tom saw an attractive girl leave the bar and approach them.

"Please excuse my boldness, but I know I've seen you before." She looked at Tom. "Do you boys live in the area?" Without waiting for an answer, she slid into the booth on the opposite side of where they were sitting.

Tom spoke first, "Honey, that is the worst pickup line I've heard, and I've heard my fair share. You should try being more original."

"It's not a line. I know I've seen you before." She waved to the other girl that was with her to leave the bar and join them. "My name is Dahlia. This is my friend Naomi."

Naomi slid into the booth next to her and smiled. After a few awkward moments of silence, the girls realized they were not going to be told the names of these gentlemen. They both took out business cards and put them on the table.

"We're both lawyers. We work for a rather prestigious litigation firm in West Palm Beach. If you should ever need excellent representation, then just call us. In the meantime, I will certainly recall where I know you from." Both ladies returned to the bar.

Randy and Tom looked at each other.

"Are we missing the completion of a wonderful day?"

Early Monday morning, Sandy's cell phone rang. "Hi, Mom. Is everything okay?"

"Dear, I have to read you a portion of an article from today's newspaper. It comes straight from the gossip column. Are you ready?"

"Sure."

"Seen at the posh Green Tequila restaurant and lounge in West Palm Beach were Randolph Forester and Thomas

Bailey, enjoying themselves and chatting it up with two hot, young lovelies in a center booth."

"Mom, I'm sure that there's a valid explanation. I trust Randy to honor our commitment."

"When did you see him last, Sandy?"

"Well, not for a while. I'm determined to get my law degree, and I'm working my ass off."

"Well, dear, maybe you should rethink your priorities. I believe a Mrs. Randolph Forester degree is a lot more desirable."

"Thanks, Mom. I'll think about it."

"Tom, there is a personal phone call for you," called Paula. "Maybe you should take it in Randy's office."

"Hello, Tom here."

"I placed you. You are Thomas Bailey. We met in college. You were a senior at Wharton, and I was a senior at the University of Pennsylvania. We exchanged greetings many times. So your friend has to be your cousin, Randolph Forester."

"Dahlia, you're right. Where are you now, and how did you find me?"

"I'm in my office in West Palm with a dozen or two yearbooks on my desk, and that's where I saw your picture. I'm a pretty great lawyer, so it was easy to find you. How about you come down to West Palm on Saturday night for a nice, quiet dinner? A sort of get-to-know-each-other, and I can promise you a great dessert."

"I don't know, Dahlia. I'm sort of committed."

"Tom, after you experience the dessert I have in mind for you, your commitment will be over."

"Thank you for the invite, Dahlia. I'll be in touch."

"Well, don't wait too long, for I'll have to go to the market in the morning for some breakfast."

"Hey, Dad, when is the next board meeting? I'm going to propose some sweeping changes."

"Next Monday morning. How about faxing me a copy before so I can review it?"

"Sure thing, Dad. As long as you don't reveal anything to anyone before the meeting."

Randy then called out to Paula, "Clear your schedule. We're bringing a proposal to Monday's board meeting, and I need you to accompany me."

At the board meeting, Randy started, "Gentlemen, before I begin, you all know Paula, my operations manager. Please allow me to complete my presentation. Then we can discuss and answer any questions. If you agree, I wish to bring my division into the main company. First, the Rand division is very successful, and there is no reason to be separated. It should be part of the company. Two, it would eliminate the duplication of many similar departments, such as finance, marketing, billing, shipping, and more. However, the change will be based upon the following proposal. Grandpa, you will be board chairman emeritus. My father will assume the duties of chairman."

Pausing to swallow a huge lump in his throat, he continued, "I'll move to Atlanta into the executive office and be in charge of the entire company. I propose to bring Thomas

Bailey to Atlanta also to be the top executive manager and consolidate all the departments under his leadership.

"I propose bringing back Jack Palmer to be chief financial officer. I will offer Scott Peterson early retirement. I am bringing the Rand division into the main company because it is embarking on manufacturing and marketing a new product. I am asking Grandpa to help with this new endeavor, and with his wealth of knowledge, it will be successful.

"The new product we have just secured a patent for is a medical breakthrough. A wall-covering paint that is infused with five different antibiotics to create infection- and virus-free areas. So until the product is successful, it will be a separate Rand division."

The ensuing discussion lasted several hours and was unanimously approved.

"There is one other topic I will now bring up. We have sales representatives throughout the country that have been with Carson Forester for years. A great many of them have become lazy and rely on the reputation of the company for business instead of actually working. This will be my first review. I am confident we can increase our business substantially with new, young, energetic representatives."

The next day in Jacksonville, he outlined the new job with Tom and informed him he would receive one hundred thousand shares in Carson Forester to bond him to the family business.

He then talked to Jack Palmer. "Jack, I know you will hate to move your family again, but I am sure they will be happy to move back to Atlanta. I'm doubling your salary as of now, and I have some nice hefty bonuses in store for you."

On Sunday morning, Sandy and Joann were chatting over some breakfast.

"Joann, why are you so quiet?" asked Sandy.

"Sandy, listen to me. I have met someone. Two weeks ago, I was having lunch in the George Washington Café. A guy wearing hospital scrubs was at a nearby table alone and wouldn't stop glancing at me. A few days later, I was there again, having a cup of coffee when I saw the same guy eating lunch at another table. He looked at me and smiled. I smiled back. At that instant he picked up his tray and asked to join me, saying he hated to eat alone. Would you believe I became nervous? That has never happened to me before. He extended his hand and said his name was Roger and he was doing his residency at the George Washington Hospital. I told him my name and said I was studying for my law degree here. And as we chatted, he looked directly at me the entire time. I became aware that my heart was doing flip-flops. When we parted, he said to me that he hoped we could meet again. he said this was possibly the best lunch he'd ever had.

"A few days later, I walked into the café again. A huge lump formed in my throat as I scanned the tables. I was carrying my tray to a table when I heard his voice behind me. I turned, and he asked if we could have lunch together. Sandy, I can tell you that my heart was jumping out of my chest, and I hardly heard the conversation, but what I heard very clearly was this, 'Would you have dinner with me tomorrow evening? I am on the 8:00 p.m. to 6:00 a.m. shift at the hospital, so it would have to be early. I hope you'll say yes.' I said I'd love to. He said that we could meet at the Ale House across the street from the hospital. I said that sounded perfect since I had two evening classes that night.

"He was waiting for me at the desk in the restaurant. He took my hand, and we went into a booth. We then proceeded to feast on juicy hamburgers, gorge on a bucket of fries, and swashed everything down with sweet iced tea. We laughed and told funny stories, and we talked for what seemed like forever. Suddenly he glanced at his watch and noticed it was seven thirty. We quickly left the money on the table and ran across the street holding hands. Saying good-byes, we stood awkwardly facing each other. My mind was racing, and all I wanted was for him to kiss me. But he didn't.

"The next day I went to the cafeteria and was going to wait as long as possible to see him. And just like that, there he was. He came to me, put his arms around my waist, and forced his lips onto mine. I thought my heart was going to explode. I circled his neck and drew him into me. Then we really kissed. It was convenient that he was holding me because my knees felt like rubber.

"Now here's my dilemma, Sandy. Tom and I have been dating for almost two years, but he never made any sort of commitment. I can tell you that I'm absolutely head over heels for this man, and I know he feels the same way."

"That's remarkable, Joann!" exclaimed Sandy. "It's rather exciting because to find true love and to know in your heart is something truly spectacular. Finding something where you know that nothing else matters is just wow. I'm truly happy for you, Joann.

"But now you have to listen to me. I'm leaving law school. I can't be away from Randy. He's my true love, and I would be devastated if he met somebody else. We're engaged to be married, and I want that more than a law degree. I'm already packed, and I called Randy to pick me up and take me home. But just promise me that we will remain close friends."

Later that evening, Randy greeted Sandy. "Hi, Sandy. What's up?"

"Randy honey, after three weeks away, I realize that my life would never be complete without you. I miss you. I love you with all my heart. I want very much to begin our lives together. I thought a career was more important to me. I was wrong. What is more important is loving you. I am all packed. Please arrange to pick me up. I am coming home and into your arms."

"Sandy, I cannot tell you how I have longed to hear those words. Please promise me we will never again be separated."

"I promise," she whispered.

"Grandpa, would you allow me to share your office? I could really benefit from your vast experience, and then Dad could stay where he is."

"Randy," replied Grandpa, "that would be my greatest pleasure to come here and see you."

"Grandpa, also I need a motivated people person to coordinate all the changes here and to make sure all managers work together to do the job we require."

"Randy, I know who I would like to see in that position."

"Who, Grandpa?"

"Your cousin Alexis. She is graduating now. Vanessa called me and asked me to find her something. She is smart and worldly. And don't forget. Your Aunt Vanessa owns over 10 percent of the shares in the company."

"Grandpa, as always, you have the right answers. Could you interview her? Also speak to Dad. See if he has any objections."

A few days later, Randy heard, "Good morning, Mr. Forester. Your cousin Alexis is in your office."

Randy went to his office. "Hello, Alexis. I am really happy to see you. The last time was at the family Christmas party. You look smashing. I am always startled when I see your beautiful blue eyes."

Alexis laughed. Her shoulder-length auburn hair with blonde streaks highlighted her flawless complexion. She was wearing a honey beige business suit with a knee-length skirt. She eluded a warm confidence that really added to the attractiveness.

"Thanks, Randy. I have heard a lot of good reports of your activities. No question you are in charge."

"Alexis, I am working diligently to build a great company for the family."

Alexis spoke, "Grandpa filled me in on your proposal. I am very interested."

"Alexis, this job is no walk in the park. We have seven managers. I need you to supervise them to make sure everything is smoothly coordinated. I need someone to handle an executive position yet not make the managers less important."

"Randy, if you agree, I am sure I can do everything that you outline."

"Alexis, one more thing, your brother Tom is now the general manager, so you will work closely with him."

"No problem," she answered. "We get along very well. If a problem arises, I would defer to him, as he is my older brother."

"Okay, welcome! As your family already receives profit money, how about you start at two thousand dollars a week and see how it goes?"

"Thanks! Great. When do I start?"

"You just did. See Grandpa to arrange for an office and to take you on a tour to meet everyone."

Randy then called Paula. "Hi, Paula. I need to talk to you."

"Okay, Randy, I'll be there in a few minutes."

"Paula, please take a seat. I need to make a few adjustments to your job description. I have all approvals to build an addition to the Jacksonville plant that will be for the new medical coating manufacturing. It will still be the Rand division, but Medec is now completely separate. I need you to be in charge completely. I know you can do it as we did every step of the way together to make MajDec successful. It will be MajDec all over again, only a different product."

"Whatever you need I will provide, but again you are the boss. I also know that you would rather be in Jacksonville with your family. You will have Sam, the cars, the chopper, and the jet. All because I have the company transportation now. How about I start you with five thousand dollars a week plus benefits and earned bonuses? Just remember that you always report to me only."

"Oh my God, Randy!" cried Paula, wiping away tears. "We've been together every day for more than two years. Do you really think I can do this on my own?"

"Paula, I know you'll do great. First, I need you to work with my cousin Alexis for a little while. You are the boss of the Rand division, and I just need you to send me a weekly report. Send all the bills to Jack Palmer with a weekly report to be marked confidential."

"Tom, this is Joann. We have to talk. I tried calling you at home and was informed that your phone number was disconnected. I called Jacksonville, and some new office manager finally agreed to give me your phone number."

"Joann, where are you? What do you need to talk to me about?"

"Where I am isn't important. This is painful to do over the phone because I was always sure that we would be married and start a family. And I could always count on your quiet strength and your loving way. I believed you were right for me. But I've met a man that makes my heart pound and my body tremble. Just being with him overwhelms me. You and I had an understanding, but never a real commitment. Tom, I'm truly sorry, and I hope you can understand."

Without a word, Tom hung up the phone, put on his jacket, and made his way out of the office.

The next afternoon Randy's private phone rang.

"Hey, Alexis, how are you?"

"Have you seen or even heard from Tom?" she asked. "He left early yesterday and hasn't been to the office at all today. I'm starting to get worried because it's not like him. He isn't answering his cell phone, and there isn't an answer at his apartment."

"Just hold on, Alexis. I'll meet you in the garage in five minutes."

"I know something happened to him, Randy."

"Alexis, calm down. Let's just drive around to some of his favorite places. The coffee shop he usually stops at in the morning. The bookstore he spends his time in. Let's just cruise around town."

Suddenly, Alexis heard, "Alexis, I am your new executive assistant, Marge. Your brother is in your office, and he looks terrible."

Hurriedly returning to the office, Alexis grabbed Randy's arm.

"Please, let me handle this," he said.

"Tom, look at your clothes. What happened? What's wrong with you? You haven't shaved or combed your hair, and I can smell the booze on you. Please just tell me what happened."

Alexis listened attentively as Tom poured out his story of rejection.

And when he finished, she retorted, "You may not know this now, Tom, but she did you a favor. This could have happened when you were married. Apparently she wasn't as committed to you as you were to her. Listen, big brother. When the news gets around that Thomas Bailey is available, the ladies will be lined up with invitations to home-cooked dinners and stays for breakfast. Go home, and get cleaned up. Randy and I made reservations for the three of us at seven at the Italian Gardens. Remember that we'll always be family."

"Thank you, Sis."

Somehow word leaked out about the new medical wall paint. Paula was forced to install an automatic answering machine on the phones with an automated message, "The Rand division of the Carson Forester company has successfully tested and patented an off-white wall paint that will effectively eliminate all infections and airborne viruses in medical facilities. It is only available through authorized Carson Forester dealers. Deliveries are expected to begin approximately three months from now."

Paula then called for Randy. "Hello, Sherrie. This is Paula. Can I please speak to Randy?"

"I'm sorry, Paula, but he won't be back in the office until Monday morning. Can Alexis help you?"

"Sure! Thank you, Sherrie."

Alexis then picked up. "Hi, Paula. This is Alexis."

"Hey, Alexis, would it be possible for Tom to give me a few days? I need to purchase a ton of technical equipment. He has the experience I need, as he did all of the purchasing for MajDec."

"Absolutely, Paula. Make arrangements to pick him up here on Monday morning. I'll tell him to be ready, and good luck in your new position!"

"Thank you, Alexis. Have a wonderful day."

After a sleepless night, Sandy was nervously walking from one room to another in the apartment, just waiting for the chopper to pick her up. Glancing out the window, she saw two men walking toward her apartment building. One had on a pilot's cap and uniform, and to her surprise, the other was Randy. As she ran to the door of her apartment, she lost her balance and fell into Randy's outstretched arms like something out of a movie. For several minutes, neither one of them spoke. They just clung to each other.

"Sandy honey, we'll change to the jet in Atlanta and take you home."

"Randy," she said quietly, "this being Friday, I don't want to go home just yet."

"Oh, really, darling? Where would you like to go?"

"With all my heart, I want to go to your apartment with you until Sunday. We have a lot to discuss."

The look he gave her brought tears to her eyes, along with a torrent of love. Friday night through Saturday night, they talked, planned, laughed, and traded lots of emotional loving.

At breakfast Sunday morning, she asked, "Randy, I would like to visit your grandparents today, and then you can take me home, okay?"

Grandma and Grandpa greeted them with a great warmth. "We're so happy you came to see us."

Sitting at the kitchen table while eating Grandma's famous French toast, they discussed every issue and listened to a plethora of Grandpa's stories.

Grandpa took Sandy's hand. "I want to give you a tour of this beautiful house." Still holding her hand, he said, "This is the grand entrance foyer." He then led her down to the living room and the huge formal dining room with the beautiful walnut table that was large enough for twenty diners. The next stop was to the great room, the media room, and the beautiful breakfast room.

Grandpa continued, "We just had all the walls repainted with MajDec. Before, everything was white, and as you know, white is boring. We have difficulty climbing the stairs to the second floor, so we only go up at bedtime. There are four large bedrooms plus a huge corner master bedroom suite." He led her back to the large screened-in terrace with the deep water pool. "There is a three-car garage, and over the garage is a spacious apartment with the couple that helps us living there. They are retiring after living with us for many years and moving to Florida."

Still holding Sandy's hand, he led her back to the kitchen. "My father was a builder. He built several senior gated communities. He was very successful. He built this house for us as a wedding present. It's in the finest residential area of Atlanta. We have decided it is time for us to move to an independent living facility not far from here. So we would like to give you and Randy this house and property as a wedding present to continue the tradition."

For a moment Sandy was speechless. Then she leaned over, gave Grandpa a huge hug, and whispered in his ear, "I love you, Grandpa. Thank you." She went over to Grandma, leaned down, and kissed her.

As they left, the good-byes were very emotional.

"Hello, Vivian. This is Carol Vanderbrook. I hesitated to phone you before, but now I am sure you are aware of the new situation with the children."

"Yes, Carol, I also have hesitated calling you. We are very happy with the new development. So mother of the groom-to-be from mother of the bride-to-be, what is our next move?"

Vivian replied, "I guess we are planning a wedding. I am sure we both have already started thinking about it. Would you agree that the first project is to start a guest list so we can send out save-the-date letters."

"How about we work on our lists and agree to meet?"

"Very good, Carol. I will meet you Tuesday morning at the airport VIP lounge."

That evening after dinner, Vivian said, "Adam, I am meeting Carol Vanderbrook on Tuesday morning to discuss our guest list."

"Vivian, how many do you have on our list so far?"

"I can tell you, Adam, this is a huge undertaking. My must-invite list is over three hundred."

"My gosh!" exclaimed Adam. "That's outrageous!"

"I know, Adam. I have made separate lists of business, political, and friends and haven't even gotten to the family list."

"Listen, Vivian, we must offer to pay half of all costs," said Adam. "I know at first it may seem insulting to them, but this is the right approach. When you meet on Tuesday, be very tactful in making the offer. I'm sure you will handle this correctly."

Greeting each other on Tuesday morning, they hugged and kissed, becoming very emotional.

"Vivian, could we have our discussion here in the VIP lounge? I instructed my driver to wait for me, okay?"

"Sure, let's order some lunch and go over our lists and preliminary plans."

"Carol, before we begin, I have to discuss something of great importance with you. I have worked and reworked my lists and left out as many as possible. It is still over three hundred. So Adam and I will insist on us paying half of all costs. Please do not feel insulted, as this is very fair."

Carol gave a nervous laugh. "You are not going to believe this, but my bare list is well over three hundred. Charles has medical colleges all over the world. Over the years he has been awarded so many honors on his surgical skills, not to mention his hospital and clinic associates."

"Vivian, I really appreciate your offer. I will discuss it with Charles."

They spent the next few hours happily talking, crying, and recanting stories about the children. They parted finally as close friends.

"Dr. Vanderbrook, there is a phone call for you from a Mr. Adam Forester."

"Thank you. Please put him through on my private line."

The doctor picked up the line. "Good morning, Adam. What a nice surprise hearing from you."

"Hello, Charles. I know you are very busy, so I'll get to the point. Our wives are planning a grand wedding, and I understand the guest lists are well over six hundred. I am very hopeful that you will accept our sincere offer to pay half of all costs, as this is turning out to be outrageously expensive."

"Adam, I thank you for your generous offer. I do agree with you that this could become unbelievably expensive."

"Let's all give it some thought and discuss it with the children."

"Okay," replied Charles, "and many thanks."

"Dad, I need to talk to you for a few minutes."

"Sure, Randy. Is it serious?"

"Dad, I have to be in Jacksonville for two days next week. We are starting to manufacture the new medical paint. Paula has arranged a small ribbon-cutting ceremony and has invited many representatives of medical journals and others in the medical field to attend. She will conduct a tour of the new plant and give details of the product. Could you fill in for me in Atlanta?"

"Sure, Randy, I can do that. I understand why you want to be there as this could turn out to be a phenomenal success."

As Randy arrived at the plant, Paula rushed over very excitedly. "Look at this." She shoved a fat stack of papers at him. "We've already received orders from dealers for over twenty thousand gallons!"

"Paula, this is fantastic. I knew you could do it."

"Randy, you will never know how much I appreciate your confidence in me. Also Reza and Victor Sanchez are here. Norman could not make the trip."

"Good, I want to see them also. It is due to their inventions that we're here today."

"Hello, Dahlia. This is Tom Bailey. How are you?"

"Hi, Tom. I am happy to hear from you."

"Dahlia, is the invitation that you extended to me still good?"

"You bet it is, Tom."

"Good. If you have no other plans for this weekend, pick me up at the Palm Beach airport Saturday morning. I will meet you in the VIP lounge."

That weekend, after a nervous greeting, both were silent as they found two large chairs facing each other. Dahlia was wearing white shorts and a Marlins sweatshirt, and he noticed immediately her shapely legs with white sneakers.

"Tom, let's spend a little time getting acquainted, okay?"

He nodded. "Dahlia, first I want to say that I forgot how extremely attractive you are. I am Thomas Bailey. My parents are both very successful lawyers in the Atlanta area. I have a younger sister Alexis who just graduated from Oxford University in England as a Rhodes Scholar. I graduated from the University of Pennsylvania and then received a master's degree from Wharton. I am the general manager in my family business, Carson Forester Paint Manufacturing Company in Atlanta. You met my cousin, Randy Forester. We are best friends as well as related. Dahlia, I am not interested in getting laid and saying good-bye." Looking directly at her, he realized she had been looking intently into his eyes, absorbing his every word. As he gave a very nervous smile, he said, "Dahlia, it is your turn."

"I am Dahlia Wallace. My father is the wholesale distributor for several new automobile manufacturers with exclusive franchises and contracts for the entire Southeast. I have an older brother, Don, who is an executive in the family business. I am a litigation attorney. I graduated from the University of Pennsylvania. That's how I tracked you down. My best friend Naomi and I specialize in major litigation for the firm of Platt and Rivera in Palm Beach. If I gave you the wrong impression when we met at the Green Tequila, I apologize. That place makes you do crazy things. I am not like that, and I too am happy in a solid relationship, not a one-night wrestling match."

"Dahlia, I appreciate this conversation and would really like to spend the weekend with you. First let me check into a hotel."

"First, Tom, I have my convertible in the garage here. It is a beautiful day. Let me give you a tour of Palm Beach. We will discuss the hotel later, okay?"

Driving the length of A1A, she showed him the beauty of the area and the mansions and named who lived in them. They walked the entire Worth Avenue, stopping at the shops to admire the fantastic array of merchandise. They sat at an outdoor café, drank coffee, and shared great pastries.

It was past five o'clock when they strolled back to the car. They talked, laughed, and told family anecdotes.

Without realizing it, Tom took Dahlia's hand and held it until they reached the car. "Where are we having dinner?" he asked.

"I have dinner all prepared. I just have to heat it up. Also I invited Naomi and her on-and-off boyfriend to join us."

"That sounds wonderful. Please stop at the liquor store. I want to buy the wine."

As he came out of the store, he was carrying two large bottles, one white and the other red. He held them up and laughed. "I come prepared. Shall I change into some more formal attire?"

"No, Tom. It is come as you are."

They had barely entered the apartment when the doorbell rang.

"Hi, Naomi. Hi, Walter. Come on in. We just arrived also."

"Tom, I am sure you remember my best friend, Naomi." They both laughed and blushed.

"Good day." Naomi extended her hand in greeting.

"I would like you to meet Walter Barlow." The two men shook hands and exchanged greetings.

"Naomi, come into the kitchen. I have not even started to heat dinner." They gave each other a knowing look. "And why don't you guys open the wine?"

Tom was looking intently at Walter with a questioning look. "Tom, what's up? Why are you staring at me?"

"Walter Barlow," Tom repeated. "I have heard your name before and cannot place where. Do you live near here?"

"Yes," Walter replied. "I have a residential apartment in a waterfront high-rise on Clematis Street."

Coming out of the kitchen, Dahlia smacked Tom on the arm. "Are you playing my game, as if I can't place where I know you?"

After eating a delicious dinner and drinking lots of wine, everyone was talking and laughing.

Suddenly Tom stood and exclaimed, "My gosh! You are Walter Barlow Decorating Centers. It just hit me."

"That's me," Walter replied cautiously.

"Unbelievable, Walter. I have seen hundreds of your invoices. You own fine decorating centers here in Florida. You are a Carson Forester dealer."

Walter became very quiet. "Tom, how do you know so much about me?"

"Walter, I am the general manager of Carson Forester in Atlanta." The four of them sat silently, trying to absorb what just happened.

The girls jumped and yelled, "This is unbelievable!"

Tom continued, "I know that your purchases from us have increased 50 percent. Could you explain the great increase in the business?"

"Tom, it is simple. The demand for MajDec is unbelievable. Every gallon that I order and receive is already sold and at full price. Many of the contractor customers have offered to pay more if I would sell them extra gallons."

As they were continuing to discuss the retail paint market, the girls finally interrupted, "We will be in the kitchen cleaning up. We have coffee and a great dessert. So let's end all this business talk."

"Dahlia, I apologize," said Tom. "You are right. I just wanted to tell Walter about our new product."

Instantly Walter became alert. "What new product?"

As Tom related the details of Medec, Walter stood and began pacing the floor, his mind racing a mile a minute while thinking of vast possibilities.

"Okay, guys, coffee and killer chocolate cake is being served."

Tom began mercifully kidding the girls about the actions at the Green Tequila. The story expanded as they were recalling it. They were all wiping away tears of laughter. Then Naomi noticed that Walter was sitting on the sofa, lost in thought.

She went to him and put her arms around his neck. "We are just having some good-natured fun. It is not serious."

"I am sorry, honey," he replied. "My mind is just blown away with the product that Tom described."

Naomi sat on his lap and gave him a big kiss. "It is okay, sweetheart. I know with you that business is always first."

He lifted her, dropped her on the sofa, gently fell on top of her, and shouted, "Not if you would agree to marry me."

Dahlia sat up in shock. "Naomi, is he telling us that you are the one not saying yes and all this time as your best friend you always gave me the impression that Walter was not serious?"

There was silence.

As Tom stood, he said, "Dahlia, I really had a great time. Dinner was wonderful. You are wonderful. I will call a cab and go to the hotel."

Dahlia touched his hand. "Are you nuts? It is after midnight. I have a very nice guest room and private bath, and you are staying right here." She leaned against him and whispered, "Besides I already have everything for breakfast."

"Hi, Dad."

"Randy, what's up?"

"Dad, I have to be in Jacksonville for a few days more. Could you take my calls?"

"Sure, when you return I would like to hear a report."

Paula greeted him with a big smile. "This is MajDec all over again. I have requested dealers to fax me the orders so I will have a printed record, but the fax machine cannot keep up with the flood of orders coming in from all over the world. Also the results of our test run show that the manufacturing process takes longer than we had originally calculated. The different antibiotics are taking more time to melt into bases."

"Paula, please keep calm, as this is uncharted technology. If we cannot meet the sixty-eight dollar per gallon price, we will have to increase it. Also we pay the Boca group four dollars per gallon."

"Randy, you are right."

"Okay, Paula, let's back up. This is a product that we hold patents on. Every medical facility worldwide is clamoring for our Medec, and at the old price, the Carson Forester dealers will make more money than we will. So here is what I am telling you to do. Send out a letter to each dealer saying, 'Due to the unprecedented demand for Medec, we want you to retail this product for no less than one hundred seventy-five dollars per gallon, and your cost is now eighty-eight dollars per gallon. Please notify me if you want to cancel any or part of any orders.

"Paula, you are doing a fabulous job, but please keep calm. Remember it is very unusual that, in this case, the dealers need us more than we need them."

Chapter 7

When Randy arrived at his office Monday morning, there was a special delivery envelope on his desk. Inside was a note from Grandpa saying they had moved, along with the deed to the house and property. Grandpa wrote, "The couple that takes care of everything will stay until you and Sandy move in."

He immediately called Sandy and left her a message.

"Hello, Carol. This is Vivian. Have you and Charles made any decisions?"

"Hi, Viv. No, we're trying to figure this out. I can tell you it's overwhelming. Have you spoken about this with Sandy?"

"Yes, but her mind is in the clouds somewhere. She talks with Randy every night at length, but it is all about love."

"Okay, just let me know if anything is decided."

"Hi, Dad. I need to talk to you."

"Oh no, Randy. I haven't digested the information from the last meeting, but I must tell you that having young, energetic sales reps have paid off. Our business is up 28 percent this quarter over the last year."

"I know, Dad. I have been phoning our dealers over the past three days. They are all jumping for joy. They are making more money. The new reps are a huge help. They love the new labels and products. Medec has been a huge boost to business. However, Dad, our profit margin is not high enough. The easiest but worst decision would be to raise prices. So we need another way of bringing in more money."

"Here are my two proposals for your consideration. First, any new dealer that we approve would pay a flat entry fee of fifty thousand dollars. Second, every dealer must purchase all the sundry items, such as but not limited to brushes, rollers, all paint tools, and so forth from us. Our reps will be responsible in monitoring each of his dealers to make sure they comply. We can start with a buying group until we start production on our own."

Walking into the house while holding hands, Sandy and Randy were met by the couple that worked for Grandpa and Grandma.

"Hello, we are Mr. and Mrs. Campbell. You must be Randolph Forester, and this is, of course, your fiancée."

They shook hands, and Randy asked, "I understand that you guys are leaving?"

"Well, Mr. Forester, we would agree to stay until you move in so we can protect all the property."

"Mr. Campbell, it would really be appreciated if you would," replied Randy.

"Mr. Carson paid us one hundred dollars a week, plus we got the apartment for free. And when Mrs. Campbell did all the cooking, she would make enough for us also. We had every Sunday off, and we could use one of his cars, as I did the driving."

"Mr. and Mrs. Campbell, we would consider it a great favor if you would stay. I will pay you two hundred per week. You both can have Saturday and Sunday off. Also I am bringing a car up from Florida that I do not need. I would be happy to give it to you."

"Mr. Randolph, we are very happy here. We only decided to move because we were not sure about your plans. We gratefully accept your offer. Mrs. Campbell takes care of everything inside, and I take care of everything outside. I do the driving, the marketing, and whatever else has to be done. I am a very competent handyman."

Sandy chimed in, "Thank you both very much."

As they walked from room to room, Sandy was beaming. "This is a wonderful house, but there are some areas that I would like to remodel."

"Okay, such as?" he asked.

"I would like to break through the master suite with the adjoining room and make it larger, remodel the master bath, and add a larger walk-in closet. In the kitchen, I would like new appliances and maybe a new countertop."

"Honey, do it."

"Great!" replied Sandy. "I will call Grandpa and tell him what we are planning and ask him to recommend a general contractor."

"Absolutely. I will be here every day."

"Really? Where will you be staying?"

"I am going to stay with you. I will be here with the workman during the day, and at night, I am yours."

There was a moment of silence as they both experienced an increase in their heart rate.

The two lovers holding hands spoke simultaneously, "It's time to get our mothers together and reveal the secret plans for our wedding. The phone calls between the mothers have continued without any completed plans due to the overwhelming planning of such a large wedding."

"Hi, Mom."

"Hello, Sandy. How is the remodeling progressing?"

"Great, Mom. It is completed. We want to pick up Randy's mother, and the three of us will fly to you and discuss the wedding plans. Is that okay?"

"Hi, Mom."

"Hello, Randy. How are you and Sandy?"

"Mom, we will pick you up Friday morning. You, Sandy, and I will fly to Rumson, New Jersey, and meet with Sandy's mother to discuss our wedding plans. Is that okay?"

"Oh, yes."

After a lot of hugs and kisses, they said, "Mothers, please sit down, and we will tell you our wedding plans. First, we have to absolutely make sure that what we tell you today is a secret. The only people that will know are we. So you both have to pledge to us that you will keep our secret."

They both quickly agreed and sat nervously.

Sandy continued, "We will invite only the family to our house for a party to celebrate the completed remodeling. But what it really turns out to be is our wedding in our home. I will arrange the catering, and I will ask Grandpa's friend, Judge Atherton, to officiate."

As the mothers recovered from shock, they both started talking at once with a thousand questions.

Finally Randy said, "Enough. We love you both very much, but the insurmountable job of a public wedding is way too expensive and too difficult to plan. This is final, and please remember that you both pledged to keep our secret."

They all began arriving with anticipation of touring the home. Sandy and Randy greeted Grandma and Grandpa Forester, Vivian and Adam Forester, Vanessa and Franklin Bailey, Tom Bailey and his girlfriend Dahlia, Alexis Bailey, Carol and Dr. Charles Vanderbrook, and Dina and Dr. Byron Vanderbrook.

As everyone had finished the tour with oohs and aahs at the beautiful home, the talking, the laughter, the eating, and drinking began. Just then the doorbell rang. Sandy opened the door.

"Good afternoon, Judge Atherton."

There was a shocked silence.

Sandy held the judge's arm. "You all know the Honorable Chief Justice of the Georgia Supreme Court, Roland Atherton. He is going to marry us."

Grandpa Carson stood. "Roland, you sly dog. We have lunch together every Friday, and you never let on."

"I am sorry, Carson, but I was sworn to secrecy."

The two mothers stood beside them, trying to hold back the tears until they heard the judge's words, "Sandra Vanderbrook and Randolph Forester, I now pronounce you husband and wife."

The two mothers, with tears streaming down their faces, ran into each other's arms in a long, emotional hug. What followed was bedlam, laughter, crying, and unbelievable shock, followed by the warmest love that had joined two prominent families. No one realized that the newlyweds had left for a weeklong honeymoon. The only person that knew where they were was Randy's father, Adam.

The next day, the lead story in every newspaper and on TV was the secret wedding joining two prominent families.

Chapter 8

"Sherrie, the following letter is to be faxed to every sales representative," directed Randy. "Please attend a meeting to be held May 24 at 8:30 a.m. and lasting until 4:00 p.m. with a two-hour lunch break. A buffet lunch will served in the company cafeteria. Please contact the company travel office and make all arrangements."

"Good morning, ladies and gentleman. I am Randy Forester. Today we will cover a great many topics, and before we adjourn, the last hour will be devoted to your questions, so please make notes and present your questions then. Our first speaker will be Alexis Bailey, our senior manager, to give you an overall picture of the Carson Forester Company. The second speaker will be Thomas Bailey, who will introduce all of the division and branch managers. The third speaker will be Mr. Arnold Berger, who will give you an update on MajDec. And last but not least will be Paula, who will tell you about our newest product, Medec. Please allow me to now introduce you to Mr. Norman Springer, the inventor of our two products, and Reza and Victor Sanchez, who brought this opportunity to us."

For the next two hours, they all listened intently and took loads of notes. Then came the lunch break. A fabulous buffet was waiting in the cafeteria where the eating and conversation was nonstop.

At two thirty, Randy again stood. "I have a few remarks and an announcement. For the first time with any national paint manufacturer, our sales force includes many women, and we welcome them. As to the fax you all received regarding the sales of sundries to dealers, it will be enforced. No excuses. Second, I am sure you are aware that all Carson Forester dealers are enjoying increased profits due to MajDec, and after Medec is available, they will be in a position to reap even greater profits. The fifty thousand-dollar buy-in fee for new dealers is now in effect as well as a bonus to the sales rep that brings in a new dealer. For any existing dealer that sells his business, the buyer will be required to pay the fee. I am also announcing at this time, starting June 1, an increase of 5 percent to our commissions, which I hope will encourage you to work to increase sales."

The meeting was adjourned at four without questions, only complete satisfaction. Then at the family meeting, Adam reported that sales were up over 50 percent and praised Randy for making it happen. Randy thanked everyone for their support and announced that Alexis had agreed to assume the position of worldwide expansion efforts, but her office would still be in Atlanta. She would coordinate all global operations. Then huge bonuses were handed out to every family member.

"Hi, Sandy. I'm home."

"Randy honey, I just got off the phone with Dahlia. She and Tom have set a wedding date, and we also discussed exploring a litigation law partnership in Atlanta when she moves here."

"Wow, it sounds like a good idea. Sandy, with your radiant smile and short skirt, you will certainly sway the jury."

"Clients will agree to arbitration and, if no results, then litigation. If the defending party is unwilling to enter into arbitration, we will closely examine our client's claim. If we decide the claim is valid, we will litigate with no up-front fees. We get paid only if we win."

Randy interjected, "That should have prospective clients lined up around the block."

"Thanks, honey, but first we need an office in a high-rise commercial building. We want something very unpretentious."

Randy thought for a moment. "You know what? Call Grandpa. He is very knowledgeable about Atlanta real estate."

Sandy telephone Grandpa. "Hi, Grandpa. This is Sandy. How are you and Grandma enjoying independent living?"

"Sweetheart, it's so good to hear from you. We are well and very busy with all the interesting and enjoyable activities. Congratulations on passing the bar exam."

"Thanks! Dahlia and I have formed a partnership, and I would appreciate the opportunity to talk to you about where to locate our office."

"Sure, Sandy. Why don't you and Dahlia come here for lunch tomorrow?"

"That would be great, Grandpa."

The next day, after the hugs, kisses, and endless introductions to all their new friends, Grandpa asked, "What type of an office do you have in mind?"

Sandy replied, "We do not want a fancy office, nor a snooty receptionist with a high desk."

Grandma smiled. "Carson, how about Maria's place?"

"Perfect," replied Grandpa. "Ladies, we have the perfect location for you. We own the Charles Hotel, an older but very beautiful hotel in the heart of downtown Atlanta. It is mostly residential suites but some tourist rooms. In the lobby is Maria's Place, a coffee shop, bakery, and dining room. She rents this space. Lately however, her business has suffered because two national chain coffee shops have opened a block away."

Maria's coffee and bakery area had a long, horseshoe-shaped counter with comfortable armchairs. Her wonderful homemade baked goods kept the counter busy, but the dining room was mostly empty. The rent was a thousand dollars a month, which Maria was having difficulty paying.

"You could take over the dining room space, which is about twenty feet wide by thirty feet long, and turn it into an office. Also it has direct access from the lobby and would cost you five hundred dollars a month. We would install separate utility meters. Grandma is correct. That would be a perfect setup for you. I will call Maria and tell her you are coming to look at it. I can assure you that she will be happy because she cannot continue to pay the rent anymore."

After the meeting with Maria, everyone was happy with the new arrangement. Sandy called the contractor that remodeled her home to build everything needed to turn the space into an office. With used furniture, their office was just what they wanted. The main problem then was where to put all the plants and flowers that arrived by the truckload from family and friends.

Two months later, the Bailey Forester Law Firm opened, specializing in arbitration before litigation.

"Hello, Bailey and Forester Law Office. Sure. Come in any time."

"Hello, Bailey and Forester Law Office. Absolutely. Come in any time."

"Hello, Bailey and Forester Law Office. Would tomorrow at 10:00 a.m. be convenient? Good. We will see you then."

"Hello, Bailey and Forester Law Office. Yes, sure. How about tomorrow at noon?"

Dahlia told her partner, "Oh my gosh, Sandy. Put a message on the answering machine. Please leave your number, and we will call back as soon as possible."

"I don't know, Dahlia. That's not a very good business practice."

Just then, a tall, attractive, young lady entered.

"Can I help you, miss?" asked Dahlia.

"Yes, please. I am going to college online, and I need a job. I also want to be a lawyer, so the experience would be very good."

"What is your name?"

"I am Lexa Townley. I am nineteen years old and a very good worker."

"Lexa, fill out this application, and I will talk to my partner."

"Hello, Lexa. I am Mrs. Forester. How are you at answering the phones?"

"I am pleased to meet you both. My communication skills are excellent."

"Okay, then you have a trial period."

"Thank you so much. I really need a job. When do I start?"

"Lexa, you just did. Answer the phones, and handle each prospective client politely. Get as much information and details as possible without being intrusive, and thank them."

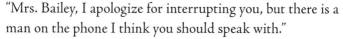

"Mrs. Bailey, I apologize for interrupting you, but there is a man on the phone I think you should speak with."

"Okay, Lexa, put him through." Dahlia then picked up the line. "This is Mrs. Bailey. Can I help you?"

"Yes, my name is Ruben Cartwright. I want to file a lawsuit against a very influential, highly regarded, extremely wealthy individual. Would you give me the opportunity of giving you the facts?"

"Absolutely, Mr. Cartwright. Could you be in our office Monday morning at 10:00 a.m.?"

"Yes, I will be there. Thank you."

Promptly at ten on Monday morning, he arrived. "Good morning. I am Ruben Cartwright. This is my wife Sharon."

"Good morning. I am Mrs. Forester. This is my partner, Mrs. Bailey."

Without hesitating Mr. Cartwright started to explain. "The BIRCH construction corporation built a luxury residential building eight stories high named the Le Grang. Each floor is a single apartment of thirty-five hundred square feet. The elevator only stops at your floor after entering a code. The top floor is the penthouse. It has an area with a raised roof completely enclosed with glass and is accessible through a rooftop patio area. The purchase price for the penthouse was ten million dollars. The couple that moved in also purchased floor seven for eight million dollars. We purchased floor six for seven million dollars. All the units sold quickly. The builder left. The seven homeowners formed an association and hired a management company and a security team.

"Two months after we moved in, the corporation that purchased the top two apartments hired an architect to design an indoor pool under the glass rooftop atrium. With the architect, they filed an application with the city for approval to start construction, and they were successful. Part of the approval was a provision to install a separate water line with meters and a separate sewer line. When the indoor pool was completed between the seventh and eighth floors, a pool maintenance company was hired, the pool was filled, and everything seemed fine. That evening my wife and I experienced burning in our eyes and then an odor from the chlorine chemical that was added to the pool water. It was so strong that we couldn't eat our dinner and were unable to sleep.

"After two weeks of unbearable chlorine odor, I called the management office because there was no way I could go to their apartment above us without the elevator code. The representative of the management company told us that we should install exhaust fans, which proved to be ineffective in a large apartment. After two weeks of unbearable odor, we were forced to move out. We had paid a two million-dollar down payment, and our bank provided a mortgage for the balance. I called the bank to discuss the problem and was told that they had bundled a lot of mortgages and sold them to an investment group. The bank manager provided us with the name of the agent that handled the sale. He informed us that the group had refinanced a lot of mortgages and sold them off in lots to other investors. So we were forced to continue paying as no one could determine who held our mortgage from our direct deposit bank account.

"As we attempted to investigate, we learned that the couple that lives in those two apartments are major contributors to political parties. Also they donate large sums to various charities and are a very large supporter of many scholarship programs and alumni fund-raising events. We spoke to the bank about the possibility of a lawsuit. I then received a phone call from a Mr. Sommers at the law firm of Clark, Jackson, and Jones. He informed me of the futile chances of a lawsuit being successful."

Both Dahlia and Sandy listened and took notes.

Then Sandy spoke first, "Mr. and Mrs. Cartwright, please give us a few days to investigate your claim, and we will phone you."

They checked through recorded deeds and spoke with many banks and loan agents, spending hours trying to determine the true owner of the apartments Forester and Bailey were finally able to convince the builder to reveal the names of the occupants. It was Perez. Finally the decision was made that the best chance of success would be to file a lawsuit against the city and the building department that approved the plans. The Cartwrights were delighted and gave their approval to the plan.

Two months later, with no reply from the clerk of courts, a letter was sent to the office of the chief judge. Again, there was no reply.

"Okay, Dahlia, what do we do now?" asked Sandy.

"Hello, Mr. Cartwright. This is Dahlia Bailey. Apparently Mr. Perez, who lives in those apartments, has friends in high places. We are being stonewalled in receiving responses to our lawsuit and letters. Perhaps you should consider retaining a more prominent and influential law firm."

"Dahlia, thank you for all you've done so far. The problem for us is that bringing action against very influential people could cost millions in legal fees. Besides having the utmost confidence in your ability to win our claim, your offer to litigate with no up-front fee and no payment unless you win is our only option."

"Okay then. We will do everything possible to bring you justice, but it could take some time."

"Thank you, Dahlia. Please do whatever you can. In the meantime, we are staying with our daughter and son-in-law, who owns a very large house, and we are certainly enjoying being together with our grandchildren."

At dinner that evening, Randy listened to the entire story and then remarked, "The only way to counter power is with power. You, my dear, are smart and educated. You have great skills and, above all, are stunningly beautiful. Perhaps you should consider filing as an independent candidate and enter the race to be the next state senator."

"Oh my God!" she shouted.

"Let's bring it up at Grandpa's birthday party in two weeks. The entire family will be here at our house. Just think, between us, the Baileys and the Vanderbrooks, we could raise millions to fund your campaign," Randy continued.

The birthday party was fabulous. The food, the good-natured joking, the laughing, and the wonderful feeling of belonging was truly evident. Randy asked for everyone's attention and told of the plan for Sandy to run for state senate. There were several moments of silence when Grandpa raised his hand.

"Dear Sandy, you are a treasured member of our family. You have made our Randy very happy, which makes us all in love with you. Over the years I have contributed to the campaigns of many powerful men. I can tell you from my personal experience that politics is a very dirty business. Why would you want to subject yourself to the filth and accusations that your opponents would invent? I am not sure you could handle it. You are too much a fabulous lady. However, if that is what you really want to do, I will support you 100 percent."

Sandy got up, went to Grandpa, put her arms around him, and gave him a huge kiss on each cheek. "Grandpa, you are so right. Dahlia and I will figure out how to represent our client."

"Also Sandy, if you wish me to, I could discuss your case with Judge Atherton on Friday at lunch," asked Grandpa.

As everyone was leaving, they were handed a shopping bag loaded with food, the desserts not eaten at the party, and the handwritten note appreciating all the love.

On Monday morning a fax was received at the law office. "You are hereby ordered to attend a pretrial hearing at 10:00 a.m. in courtroom three. Please bring your witness. Signed, Albert Johansen presiding."

"Grandpa, you are too much!" Sandy laughed.

"Mrs. Forester, please state your claim."

"Your Honor, please allow me to introduce my client, Ruben Cartwright, and Mr. Emilio Vasquez, a professor of chemistry at the Florida Atlantic University in Boca Raton."

"Thank you, Mrs. Forester. It is your turn, Mr. Sommers."

"Thank you, Your Honor. I am John Sommers, chief of litigation for the firm of Sommers, Clark, Jackson, and Jones. We are the law firm of record for the city of Atlanta, and I have decided that this claim has absolutely no merit, so I did not bring any witnesses."

"Mrs. Forester, you may proceed."

"My client, Mr. Cartwright, will testify that chlorine odor from the indoor pool above them is overbearing. Mrs. Vasquez will testify that chlorine is a gaseous element with a strong pungent odor. It is a bleaching agent used in gas warfare in World War I. When released, it sears the membranes of the nose, lungs, and throat and can cause pneumonia. There are only two resolutions to our claims. One, the building department rescind the approval and only be responsible for our legal fees, allowing my client to move back into his home. Two, the city will be liable for over seven million dollars, the price my client paid for the apartment plus our legal fees."

"Mr. Sommers, this being a pretrial hearing, what is your reply?" asked the judge. Banging his gavel, he asked, "What is the disturbance at the door, Bailiff?"

A couple entered the courtroom. "Your Honor, please excuse this interruption. I am Ralph Adamson, and this is my wife Jean. We purchased the fifth-floor apartment for five million dollars and now wish to join Mrs. Forester's claim, as we have been forced to vacate the apartment due to the effects of the chlorine odor."

Sandy motioned them to her table, shook hands, and proceeded. "Your Honor, in light of this new allegation, our claim has substantially increased. I wish to urge Mr. Sommers to think carefully regarding his reply."

"Your Honor," replied the bailiff, "there is a gentleman that wishes to speak to Mrs. Forester, and he says it is critical to her claim."

"Your Honor, please excuse this interruption. My name is Juan Perez. My wife and I purchased the seventh- and eighth-floor apartments for eighteen million dollars. I received approval from the city to install an indoor pool, which is the cause of these complaints. I wish to ask Mrs. Forester to allow me to join her in suing the city. The approval was a mistake. The officials should have investigated the effects of chlorine with an indoor residential pool. My wife and I also had to vacate our home."

Sandy waved them over. "Your Honor, may I have a few minutes to confer, please?"

"We will take a brief recess."

Sandy resumed, "Your Honor, we now have a new proposal. If the city would rescind the approval, they could rebuild Mr. Perez's apartment to the standard it was before. Mr. Perez has as estimate of two hundred thousand dollars in expenses and legal fees. We would abandon all claims, and everyone could move back into their homes. Otherwise the claim against the city is now over thirty million dollars."

Judge Johansen looked at Mr. Sommers, as Sandy continued, "We need to add the agreement that the work be completed within thirty days with a ten thousand-dollar a day penalty if not."

"Mr. Sommers, what say you?"

"Your Honor, we accept proposal number one."

The next day, all the major newspapers and TV news broadcasts proclaimed the brilliant victory of the Bailey Forester Law Firm. Mr. and Mrs. Thomas Bailey, along with Mr. and Mrs. Randolph Forester, celebrated that evening.

Randy asked, "Now that you ladies have achieved great notoriety, how about you favor Tom and me with again being loving wives?"

They laughed until they realized he was serious. So most of that night was reckless abandonment and passionate lovemaking.

The next morning Randy and Tom looked at each other blurry-eyed, laughed, and hugged. A phone call on Randy's private line interrupted them.

"Honey, Dahlia and I need to speak to you and Tom. If we could come to your office now, could you both have a few minutes?"

"Sure."

Once they arrived, they explained, "The lesson that became clear to us is because of our experience with the Cartwright trial. Women across America are at a disadvantage. Men always are more important and have more influence. We could not get a trial date without Grandpa. We truly believe that the time has come to mobilize a women's movement politically to attain the respect we deserve.

"Dahlia and I wish to organize a women-only political empowerment campaign to increase the influence of women. We have the opportunity to purchase a national TV network. We will seek only the help of millions of American women. We will enter the political primary contests across the country with a slate of distinguished women to seek election in every state, city, and town, along with houses of Congress. Any women interested in joining our movement, please contact www.thechange.gov, or phone when our headquarters are established. We need volunteers for the many divisions of our campaign such as businesses, professionals, housewives, and students in religious, medical, legal, education, and more fields. It is time for the American women to show our leadership abilities. In a few days, we will have banking in place to receive donations to fund our campaigns."

"Wow," both husbands exclaimed. "We will start you with a major donation."

"Sorry, guys. This is by and for women only."

Chapter 9

"Hi, Dad. Could we meet at Grandpa's? I have to tell you about a new development."

"Sure, Randy. How about we meet there for lunch tomorrow? Is that okay?"

"You bet it is."

"Great, and Sandy sends her love, and we can talk over lunch."

Grandpa eyed Randy. "Why are you so nervous? It is not like you."

"Well, you two are also going to be nervous when I tell you the reason for this visit. I have received a serious offer of fifteen billion dollars to purchase Carson Forester. It is an all-cash offer from a major competitor of ours, a public company, the Norwalk Thompson Group."

There was silence, and then Grandpa spoke, "As I am no longer active in the management, I will leave the decision to you both."

A lively discussion ensued, and the only agreement they arrived at was to keep this a secret and meet again in few days.

"But Randy, do you have this in writing?"

"Yes, Dad, I also have a preliminary contract with the offer."

That night, Sandy asked, "Randy honey, what is troubling you? It's been a long time since I saw you so restless. Please talk to me."

Sandy listened intently but was smart enough not to offer an opinion. The next two days, Randy was in Adam's office with the door closed, and the secretary had explicit instructions to not disturb.

Alexis entered Tom's office. "Big brother, any idea what is going on?"

"No," replied Tom, "but we can be sure it is important. From my experience with Randy, it has to be something big."

The following Monday morning at a gathering of all Carson Forester executives and reporters from all major news companies, Randy made the following announcement, "The Carson Forester Manufacturing Company founded by my grandfather of the same name has been acquired by the Norwalk Thompson Group. All present employees will be retained except the family members. The new management will determine this."

The business media worldwide dissected and discussed every detail for days. The Forester family decided not to be interviewed, which was a great disappointment for the TV news segments.

Adam called for a meeting with the Foresters, the Baileys, and the Vanderbrooks. A detailed report was distributed to all present. There were lively questions and discussions. Then the talking began on a more personal level, questioning each other as to what path would be next. However, no one was quite sure, and a nervous feeling was evident.

Adam distributed huge checks to each family member and announced, "As we all consider the Vanderbrooks as part of the families, they would also receive a generous check."

Then there was silence as everyone was in serious thought of the future.

Randy asked for attention. "I now have a proposal for your consideration."

"Oh no!" was the general retort followed by laughter.

Grandpa spoke up, "We may chuckle when Randy has a proposal, but we would not be in this measurable position if it were not for Randy's proposals." Then loud applause followed. "Now hear me out. As we know, the Panama Canal has expedited the travel time for shipping traffic between the Atlantic and Pacific Oceans. The logical destination would be in Central Florida. Good weather with a large pool of labor close proximity to the Americas. And it's being enlarged as we speak.

"There is a tract of land totaling one hundred and twenty acres, zoned as industrial. A rail line is close and could provide a spur, and it is also on a major north-south highway. My proposal is to lease, not purchase, this land and develop an industrial and storage park built to suit tenants. I estimate it will require an initial investment of approximately five million dollars. Any prospective tenant would be carefully evaluated. So give it some consideration and let me know if you wish to participate in the development of the Carson Forester Industrial Park."

Adam spoke up, "How would you proceed?"

"Dad, I would find a reliable, experienced industrial construction company. Next I would find an outstanding commercial real estate broker, but it would be our responsibility to supervise and supply the funds needed."

"Grandpa, do you have anything to add to the proposal?"

"Yes, Randy, count me in for one million."

"Randy, I am also in for a million," replied Adam.

"How about you, Tom?" asked Randy.

"Yes, and count me in for one million."

Dr. Charles Vanderbrook raised his hand. "Randy, if you would include Byron and me, we would also like to be included for one million."

"With my one million, we can now proceed. I will ask the Bailey Law Firm to prepare all the necessary documents. I will inform the business community that the Carson Forester Development Company is open for business."

"Randolph!"

"Oh no!" replied Randy. "Should I apologize now or wait to hear and then apologize?"

"No need to, honey. I want us to go to the Breakers Hotel in Palm Beach for a weekend to relax, eat, drink, play golf, and have nonstop loving."

"Terrific. When do you want to leave?"

"Tomorrow morning. Early."

"Good afternoon, Mr. and Mrs. Forester. Your suite is all prepared. Is there anything I can do for you?"

"Yes." Sandy laughed. "Please make an eight o'clock dinner reservation for us at the Green Tequila so I can get my husband in the mood."

The scene at the restaurant that evening was better than a Broadway show. After a few drinks and an outstanding dinner, they were really enjoying the atmosphere. They returned to the hotel and entered the lobby.

Randy whispered, "Honey, walk closely in front of me to the elevator because I have a huge erection that I need to hide."

Sandy backed into him and patted his erection as they both laughed. In the suite, they agreed to do the foreplay later.

Every day was glorious with eating, drinking, golfing, and having tons of sex. Both of them were upset that the weekend flew by too soon and vowed to return soon.

A management company was hired. A construction company was in place and began the installation of the water and sewer. Electricity and complicated communication equipment was being installed. Concrete was pouring daily for curbs and sidewalks. Asphalt was in place for the roads. The rails siding and tracks were underway.

While Tom was observing all the activity, a cheerily good-natured Randy startled him.

"Hi, Tom. What's up?"

"Well, a Mr. John Baker of the Tri-State Commercial real estate brokerage company has contacted me. He wishes to present a proposal for a large prospective tenant."

"When would you like to arrange the meeting? Please investigate the reputation of this brokerage company, and we will meet only in their offices. So let me know when. Also Tom, I have to compliment you. This place is humming with activity, and you have everything under control."

"Thanks, Randy, and now we have the possibility of our first tenant."

———◆———

"Gentleman, I am John Baker, agency broker. Thank you for the opportunity to present the details of a prospective tenant. Two of our sales associates, Lois Jordan and Malcom Berger, also join us. We will show you preliminary architectural drawings, aerial photos with descriptions of the space, and improvements needed. Then, if there is any interest in negotiating, we will provide complete financials, proof of affordability, and the personal history of the principals.

"This proposal calls for the leasing of the entire park, erecting a one hundred- by five hundred-foot building with fifty-foot-high ceilings and heavy-duty concrete floors. There will be three separate buildings for offices, a commissary, and parking for three hundred cars."

Tom replied, "This is a very impressive proposal. I don't know if we are able to undertake such a large project. I will call a meeting of our partners and let you know. Thank you, Mr. Baker, for your proposal."

As Tom presented the details to the partners, a spirited discussion ensued.

Finally Randy said to Tom, "I know from your presentation that you are very enthusiastic about accepting this proposal; however, I feel it is too costly and not in our best interest to lease the entire park to one tenant. However, if the majority wants to consider it, so be it. Grandpa, what is your opinion?"

"I don't have one yet," he replied. "First, we will be borrowing a huge amount of money, based on our tenant's ability to pay. I think it would be better to have many smaller tenants to spread the risk."

Charles put his arm around Tom and spoke quietly, "Tom, I think it's too risky."

Adam and the others also agreed and said, "We are not in any rush to complete this project. We don't need the money, and we all appreciate your wonderful work."

"Randy, Randy!" yelled a very excited Tom. "Hear this. A French investment fund has purchased the land that we hold the lease on and wish to negotiate buying out our lease."

"Okay, Tom, don't get too excited. If we do agree to sell, the price would be very high."

"All right, Randy, what should be my reply?"

"First, we don't need to sell. Second, we have invested around six million dollars of our own money and borrowed another ten million for the improvements. Calmly inform them that we would sell our lease for thirty-six million dollars, all cash."

"My God, Randy! That's an outrageous number. Should we call a partners' meeting?"

"Not yet. Give them the answer and see what happens. Do not negotiate. I'm sure the partners will be happy."

An hour later, Tom said, "Randy, you did it again. The deal is done."

"Great. Meet me at the lobby of the Monterey. We will have lunch and then move to the lobby to talk. Randy, I need to speak at length with you."

Chapter 10

"Good afternoon, Mr. Forester."

"Hello, John. I would like you to meet my cousin, Thomas Bailey."

"My pleasure, sir. I have reserved a corner table for you."

Both enjoyed the deluxe hamburgers with sweet potato fries and frosty beers. The discussion was mostly updating each other on all of the past events, the realization of the mutual affection. They discussed the girls' successful law firm and many family matters to be mutually understood and remarked that they were the only family members who were not going to retire.

"That is so right. Tom and I have been giving a lot of thought to another project. Here is what I propose." They both broke out in laughter.

***

Sandy and Dahlia sat in their desks in complete amazement. Every bank across the country was authorized to receive donations and then deposit in the Campaign to Advance Women's Leadership Politically. The money was literally pouring in at an astounding rate. The banks were assigned special areas to receive the money—millions of ones, fives, tens, and twenty-dollar bills. Major donors were handled personally.

"We need help!" they both exclaimed. "This is way beyond our capabilities. We need to find an outstanding leader."

After several days of constant researching and contacting different parties, the name of Amelia Donaldson reoccurred. She was an outstanding professor of politics. She was the one. They were sure. Soon under Amelia's leadership, a national headquarters was established in DC.

As staff was put in place across the country in every state, city, and town, storefront offices were opened with eager volunteers. The wave of enthusiasm was sweeping every corner of the United States. Millions of women had a new feeling of making a difference at every level in their lives. Suddenly women were walking taller, speaking out, and experiencing a new feeling of self-assurance. The dollars continued to pour in. There was no stopping this momentous event, and Amelia Donaldson was a true inspiring leader.

"Just listen, Tom. There are several large underdeveloped tracts of land in Palm Beach County, Florida. Let's explore the possibility of building a new town. We could create a concentration of garden apartments, villas, townhomes, a downtown shopping area with selective stores, a golf course and clubhouse, tennis courts, and an outdoor pool. We could also consider a high-rise for independent seniors with senior activities, amenities, and dining rooms."

As the discussion continued, many new ideas evolved for a community center, police and fire station, and schools.

Finally Randy said, "Enough speculating. Let's call a family meeting to see if there is an interest."

"Would you be willing to share the cost of preliminary drawings to show everyone?" asked Tom.

"Yes, good idea. Make an appointment for me to meet with the Gaylord firm of architects. Also I am planning a family birthday celebration for Sandy. Then would be a good time to reveal our plan."

———◈———

Everyone was in good spirits, laughing, eating, and drinking. A huge cake was wheeled in, and as everyone was loudly singing the happy birthday song, Alexis arrived with a young man. After lots of hugs and kisses, Alexis introduced Jason Wilder and apologized for being late as they had just arrived from London and the plane was delayed.

"Everyone, please give us your attention. Jason and I are considering marriage; however, we have a huge problem. I want us to return here and be a part of the family that I miss terribly. Jason is a third generation of the Wilder family, which has amassed a fortune in London real estate holdings, which Jason manages. So while we are deeply in love and committed to each other, I want to live here, and he is heavily involved in London. Also there is another factor. I am in my third month of pregnancy."

There was a stunned silence until Grandma said, "That is wonderful, Alexis, and finally I am to be a great-grandmother."

All the women began talking at once; however, the men were silent, which was not lost on Jason.

Randy and Tom rose. "May we have your attention, please? We have a proposal to present to you."

Everyone laughed and exclaimed, "Oh no! Not again."

They brought out the drawings and presented the facts. The discussion that followed was brisk, and questions and discussions were flying. Jason was keenly interested and closely examined all the drawings.

Tom tapped Randy on the shoulder and whispered in his ear, "Look at Jason. He is bursting to get involved but is hesitating."

"Jason, what's your opinion?" asked Tom.

Jason jumped to his feet quite excited. "I say jolly good. You have a first-rate idea. You build and sell or rent the commercial areas, and much more could be added to increase the revenue. And thank you for asking me. Also if you decide to go ahead with this project, perhaps you would consider including me."

Looking directly at Grandpa, Randy asked, "Before we vote, I know we would all appreciate Grandpa's opinion."

"Sure, Randy, I like the proposal, I like the project, and I like the location. The concern I have is getting all the approvals needed is a daunting task and could take years of frustrating applications. And meetings would start with the senior, and if you make it sixty-five years and older, you would not need schools right away. You could also add a medical center. I believe the entire project has a great chance of success if done slowly."

"Thanks, Grandpa. As usual, you have given us sound advice. We can start with four-story buildings, and as sales progress, we would continue to build more buildings. We would build a large activity center that could be enlarged, complete with a residents' dining room. Leave a lot of space between buildings with lakes that would flow between. So let's take a vote to see who would like to participate."

"Grandpa."

"Yes."

"Dad."

"Yes."

"Franklin."

"Yes."

"Dr. Charles."

"Yes."

"Byron."

"And I vote yes."

"Alexis, are you in?"

As she brushed away tears, she answered, "Living in Europe, attending college, and then moving back to London after the sale of Carson Forester, I realize we are a small but fiercely loyal family. I also realize that I cannot be happy unless I am part of it all. I am fortunate to have met Jason, my true love. I would be a mental disaster and could not live without him. But I cannot be happy being apart from my family. So if you would accept Jason as part of our family and if he would agree that we would divide our time between London and Atlanta, it would make me very happy to marry him if you would include us both in the family and your projects."

Jason slid off his seat and, on one knee, exclaimed, "Alexis, would you grant me the greatest honor to be my wife?"

Alexis held his arms as he stood, and then her arms went around his neck as they hugged and kissed as everyone applauded.

Jason turned and faced everyone. "This is the happiest day of my life. I am hopelessly in love with Alexis and soon to be a father. I would like to tell you the wedding will be in

Aberdeen, Scotland, in the Grampian Mountains, very near to Balmoral Castle. My family owns a beautiful villa and gardens there, and you, your friends, and all your associates are all invited as my guests. Please include me in all the future family projects."

So Carson Village Senior Community was born.

On leaving, Randy and Tom approached Jason. "We want to welcome you. We are an unbelievably close family and tell you seriously that we are in love with our beautiful Alexis and are committed to protect her in every way."

Jason was so deeply moved that all he could say was, "Thank you. You have no worries."

"Also Jason, if you are free tomorrow, we would like to give you a tour."

"Yes, I would like that very much."

"Okay, we will pick you up at 9:00 a.m. at the rooftop helipad atop the hotel where you are staying."

The next morning, they greeted him warmly and handed him the hearing device so they could communicate over the noise of the chopper. The pilot signaled, and they took off.

"Jason, we will circle the city of Atlanta so you can get an idea of its size. Atlanta is the largest city and capital of Georgia. There are many assembly plants and business headquarters located here as well as one of its busiest airports in the United States. If you look to your left, you will see the office complex of Carson Forester. If you look left again, you will see the building that is being constructed in the Carson Industrial Park, which we just sold."

"Randy, could we land next to the building that is under construction, as I would like to get a closer look at the property?"

"Sure, these buildings house the water and sewer equipment. The building on the left is all the power telecommunications. All the lines are underground. On the right is the maintenance building."

As they walked into the main building, Jason stood, silently concentrating on the construction in progress.

Randy interrupted his thoughts, "Whenever you are ready, we will fly over the store and laboratory where the new paint products were invented."

"Sure, just give me a few more minutes."

Standing quietly, a concentrating Randy asked, "What are you looking at?"

Jason replied, "Is it my imagination, or is the concrete floor not level?"

Startled, both Randy and Tom replied, "It looks perfectly even to us."

"I am sorry, guys. It is probably my imagination, but I have supervised many concrete floors being poured, and I see a problem."

Eating lunch back at the hotel, Jason gave them a rundown of his family and their accomplishments. He spoke in a nonboastful way, very unpretentious. He described his two brothers, their wives and children, and the family holdings and enormous wealth. Then they spent another hour swapping hilarious family stories. It was nearly four o'clock when Alexis and her mother entered the dining room, followed by a porter loaded with shopping bags.

"Hi, fellows. We hope you had as much fun as we did!"

The next two months were extremely busy with architects, construction, contractors, and city approvals. Every detail was working out beautifully.

"Mrs. Bailey, there is a Margaret Wilder calling for you."

"Hello, this is Vanessa Bailey."

"How do you do, Mrs. Bailey? I am Mrs. Wilder, Jason's mother. I thought I would be hearing from you sooner regarding the wedding plans."

"So good to hear from you, Margaret. I have been trying desperately to receive a date and any information from Alexis and Jason without success. I know time is of the essence, as Alexis is in her fifth month."

"Excuse me, Mrs. Bailey. Only my close friends and husband call me Margaret. Please call me Mrs. Wilder. I have to take this other call." And she hung up.

Vanessa was silent for a moment. "Wow!" she exclaimed.

When Alexis informed Jason of the call, he called her immediately. "Hello, Mother, I just became aware of your phone call with Alexis' mother. What happened?"

"Jason, when are you coming home? We have a lot to talk about. And Mrs. Bailey called me by my first name, not Mrs. Wilder. I felt that was quite improper."

"Mother, the Baileys and Foresters are one of the most respected families in the US, and both are listed among the Fortune 100. You were not talking to a housewife. Vanessa Bailey is a respected attorney. Please call her back and apologize."

"Mrs. Bailey, there is another call for you from Margaret Wilder."

"Thank you. Wait five minutes. Then ask her to please hold."

"Hello, Mrs. Wilder. This is Vanessa Bailey."

"Vanessa, this is Margaret Wilder. Please accept my humble apology for me being so rude as we are about to become in-laws. I must get used to not being so formal. Please excuse my previous conversation."

"Your apology is accepted, and we are all looking forward to meeting you and your family. Regarding any wedding plans, I do not have any information, and I can tell you that they spend every minute of the day and night together, kissing, hugging, and doing I can only imagine what else."

"Vanessa, I was just informed that Jason is returning home without Alexis, so you will probably be closer to the situation. We send our congratulations. Please keep me informed, and so will I with you. And thank you. Good day."

<hr />

"Randy, I hope you are sitting down with a large vodka on ice as I have some news. Jason was right. Here is what happened. The Aero building was completed. The tenant began moving in. The assembly lines and tracks, then the very heavy cranes, and the assembly equipment. After it was installed, they did a test run of moving the overhead cranes along the assembly line tracks. The installers heard a sharp crack but continued the test run. Then there was another sharp cracking noise. All work was halted as the installers realized the concrete floor was beginning to show large cracks. The foreman ordered everyone to clear the building. By the time they all reached the overhead doors, the walls also started to show cracks. The building inspectors were called, and they condemned the building as unsafe.

"A U.S. representative of the French investment firm was notified. He attempted to speak with the general contractor without success. A visit to his family home revealed that he and his family had suddenly moved out. The house was empty. The police were called, and a bulletin was issued to locate them. Mr. Hayes, the owner of the architectural firm was called, as his contract included supervision. Several on-site meetings were authorized with construction experts.

"Randy, listen to the results. The land was formally a landfill, and any buildings erected on it required pilings hammered deep into the ground until solid footing was established. The heavy steel grids were to be installed to support the heavy equipment in the concrete. An examination of the financial records reveal that pilings and steel was ordered and paid for. The contractor received payment for the material, but it was never installed. Meanwhile the building was condemned, and the contractor was nowhere. Then the owner of the architectural company suffered a massive heart attack and died. Fortunately we had insisted on complete payment, so we are not involved."

Sandy, realizing he was in deep in thought after hearing the sequence of events, remarked, "In a situation like this, there is no one available to sue, so investors have suffered a total loss except if the architect has assets."

The next few days, the four of them—Sandy, Dahlia, Randy, and Tom—discussed the possibility of repurchasing the project; however, the answer was evident: leave it alone.

"Hello, Tom, can you bring me up-to-date on our senior project, please?"

"Hi, Randy, yes. We now have all the necessary approvals. The plans are finalized. I have rented a trailer and had it outfitted for an office. Road directions are in place as well as a large sign next to the trailer reading, 'Welcome to the Carson Senior Villages.' I have also hired a public relations firm to staff the office and to mail brochures to prospective retirees. I am flying there Monday morning to check on everything. Would you like to go with me?"

"Sure."

As the chopper was landing, they observed many cars in front of the trailer. The area was beautifully landscaped with paved parking spaces and attractive signs everywhere.

A young lady approached them. "Welcome to the Carson Senior Villages. My name is Patricia. May I show you the models of the different buildings and locations?"

"Hello, Patricia. I am Randy Forester, and this is Tom Bailey. We are the owners of this project."

"How wonderful! I am pleased to meet you both," she replied. "I am the office manager. As you see, we have four telephone desks, and as you can observe, all phones are busy. The volume of calls is unbelievable. If you will follow me into the next office, we have set up desks with comfortable chairs for discussions with prospects. In this third room is a waiting room to talk to a trained salesperson. And as you can see, there are over ten couples waiting in addition to the people already in discussion with salespeople. The end room is the mailroom for sending out brochures and receiving inquiries. We opened a week ago and already have over five hundred applications to purchase. However, we were not authorized to accept deposits."

"Patricia, thank you for a job well done. You have everything under control, and please accept our compliment.

Tom and I will hail a cab and discuss how to finalize sales and accept deposits, and we will return after lunch."

Leaving the trailer, two men carrying briefcases approached them. They had gotten out of a stretch limo.

"Could you please tell us who the principals are of this project?"

"Why are you asking?" replied Randy.

"It is a financial matter, and we prefer speaking only with the owners or a representative."

"Well, we are the owners," replied Randy. "Would you please identify yourselves and show some ID?"

"My name is Roger Burke, and this is John Lewell. We represent the Blue Corners investment fund. We are here to investigate the possibility of purchasing this project and then report to our principals."

"Gentlemen, we were just on our way to lunch. Would you join us as our guests? We will discuss this."

"That would be great," Roger replied. "We can use our limo."

"Please instruct the driver where to take us."

"Driver, do you know where the Breakers Hotel is?"

"Yes, sir."

After a lot of questions from all and getting acquainted, Roger and John began revealing pertinent information regarding the principals of the investment firm.

Randy spoke seriously, "We would consider the following deal. We have approval for ten buildings of four stories high. Two hundred and fifty apartments of various sizes plus the usual common elements, including a large clubhouse. We would sell you one building at a time, which would protect us both. If you decide not to continue, we will have the option to, but if you wish, you can purchase more buildings, one at a time. Each building you purchase, you will be responsible for the common elements; however, we would make a separate deal for the clubhouse. Should you elect not to continue, we will have our option. The price would be four million for each building and complete payment at closing."

"Mr. Forester, Mr. Bailey, please give us a little time to phone our principals."

When they left the table, Randy asked Tom, "What is your opinion?"

Randy replied, "Tom, as usual, that was only brilliant if we break down our investment in this project. We have less than one million for each building, except the value of the approvals."

Twenty minutes later, the two men returned with a faxed offer to purchase.

"Excellent. Please have your attorney contact Charles Bailey at his law firm in Atlanta to prepare contracts."

Chapter 11

It was a beautiful September morning in Palm Beach, Florida, with bright sunshine, a clear blue sky, a few lazy clouds, and a light breeze from the ocean. He drove south on route A1A, passing magnificent newly built houses or remodeled mansions, many with large hurricane-proof windows facing the Atlantic Ocean.

Strolling out in a large veranda after an hour with her personal trainer was Annabelle Vanderbrook. A uniformed server immediately brought a small glass of chilled, freshly squeezed orange juice and a steaming hot mug of coffee with a slice of whole wheat bread lightly toasted and buttered. Annabelle was the last living member and sole heir of her family's vast chain of luxury hotels founded by her grandfather, Andrew Vanderbrook.

The St. Charles Hotels were not only famous worldwide for catering to the super rich, but also the land owned by the family was choice real estate locations, as it was privately owned. Revealing any private information to the public was not required.

Andrew's only son, Andrew Jr., who had a well-deserved reputation for wild escapades, almost always accompanied by a beautiful woman, took off from Palm Beach International Airport bound for Newark, New Jersey. Alone while piloting a newly purchased jet, he tragically crashed somewhere over Virginia. Rescue crews recovered his body and most parts of jet several days later. The crash was still under investigation by the FAA.

From a hidden pocket of her sweat suit, Annabelle put a cell phone on the table and tapped it lightly.

"Good morning. Thank you for calling. This is the main office of the Bailey and Forester Law Firm. How may I direct your call?"

The firm was a highly respectable law center with offices in Palm Beach, Miami, Atlanta, and Newark. Also it had connections to the prestigious Bailey Law Firm in Atlanta. Their client list were the movers and the shakers of the country. They had the best and brightest employees and lawyers, most graduates of the George Washington University Law school in DC.

"Yes, please. This is Annabelle Vanderbrook. I wish to speak with Mr. Edwin Rogers."

Edwin Rogers was the managing partner for the entire firm.

"Hold, please."

"Good morning, Miss Vanderbrook. This is Lexa Towney. I will connect you now."

"Hello, Belle," boomed Edwin. "How the hell are you? What a delight to hear from you."

"Cut the you-know-what, Ed. How about meeting me for lunch today?"

"Sorry, sweetheart, not today. I am too busy with appointments."

"Well then," she asked, "how about dinner tonight?"

"Okay, Belle, dinner it is."

"Ed, pick me up at eight o'clock."

"I will make reservations at the Green Tequila."

"Great. Wear something sexy to get me in the mood for that place."

The chauffer brought the limo to a stop at the entrance of the Green Tequila. A uniformed doorman rushed over to open the car door. There was an audible intake of breath from the bystanders waiting to enter.

A pair of shapely legs with shiny black patent leather high heels emerged, followed by Annabelle wearing a pure white, very short skirt with gold threads entwined in the fabric. She wore a pure white blouse with short puff sleeves, very low cut and revealing. Her blonde hair cascaded down to her shoulders. Her spectacular beauty had everyone's attention.

The long bar of gleaming mahogany had every seat taken. Many were standing, holding drinks. Young men and women were dressed in the latest fashions of expensive casual. As usual, there was an aura of sex in the air mixed with the conversation and bold body language.

"Good evening, Miss Vanderbrook."

"And a very good evening to you, Mr. Rogers."

After they were seated, a waiter in a tuxedo appeared. "May I take your drink order, please?"

"Sure," replied Edwin. "Two green tequilas. Thank you, sir."

They looked at each other for a moment and began speaking quietly as their eyes met and sparkled with the joy of being together. The attraction was evident. Their legs touched gently, massaging under the table. Edwin was having difficulty concentrating on the conversation.

Annabelle signaled for a waiter. "Please bring me a large cloth napkin." She tucked the napkin into her low-cut blouse.

"Ed dear," she said, laughing, "as you cannot take your eyes off my breasts, I am covering them so you can look in my face. I promise you that, after dinner, we will go to my home and I will gladly surrender."

As they were telling personal, funny anecdotes, their eyes looked on each other with pure joy.

They were startled when the waiter asked, "Would you care for an after-dinner cordial?"

They erupted with laughter when they realized they had eaten dinner.

In her oversized, comfortable California-style bed, they began to slowly, tenderly, meaningfully, and very satisfying make love. Afterward they held each other, not wanting to let go of this wonderful moment.

It was after midnight. Annabelle stepped furtively from her home, very quietly so as not to wake any of her staff. She was dressed in men's baggy pants that were dirty and too long with large grease stains. She wore a dirty sweatshirt. Over that was a dirty, grease-stained jacket with large pockets. She also had on heavy-duty men's work boots stuffed with socks to make them fit. In her left hand was a spray can of mace; in her right pocket was a small loaded revolver with a silencer already attached.

She slowly walked into town toward a park, passing a few homeless people. In the park, she began searching, looking everywhere and raising cardboard boxes that covered sleeping bodies. She looked under newspapers, scanning on and under benches. Then she slowly walked into dark alleys, checking out silent people scrambling in restaurant dumpsters. Searching everywhere, finally with a sigh of resignation, she returned home.

At eleven o'clock the next morning, leaning lightly on the arm of Admiral George Singleton, Annabelle dressed in a bright red pantsuit with matching high-heeled shoes. She also wore a waist-length gold jacket with red matching trim and no buttons. On her head was a wide-brimmed hat with red and gold flowers printed on the top.

The admiral was resplendent in an all-white uniform with lots of gold braids on the shoulders, sleeve, and cap. He escorted her to the line of dignitaries already assembled, including high-ranking government officials, doctors, and medical personnel. It was the groundbreaking ceremony of the Patricia and Andrew Vanderbrook hospital for the treatment of children of war veterans. It was also located in the western part of Palm Beach County on fifty acres that also was included in the donation.

Annabelle gave a smart speech to the assembled crowd. There were many reporters with cameras flashing, clicking every move of her beauty. She spoke in memory of her wonderful grandparents. "I dedicate this hospital to treat children of all veterans for free."

Then with a gold shovel, she touched the ground. As everyone applauded, she and George Singleton walked away together.

She whispered in his ear, "George, now that you are legally divorced, please come home with me. We will have leisurely lunch and then passionate sex."

He looked at her and tightened his arm holding her hand.

It was after midnight. Annabelle quietly walked out the front door, dressed as the other night. She entered the park, searching and looking everywhere. Suddenly she saw him, a young man sitting on the ground, leaning against a bench. His eyes were glazed and sunken. He had hallow cheeks and dirty, matted hair. He wore torn clothes. He sat motionless, obviously in a drug-induced stupor. Annabelle reached down, opened his jacket, and slipped a hundred-dollar bill into an inside pocket. She turned, wiped tears from her eyes with her sleeve, and returned home.

On Saturday at noon, Annabelle emerged from her limo, wearing an all-white pantsuit with gold trim, gold high-heeled shoes, and a white sailor hat with gold trim. She was greeted by Walter Johnson, who escorted her past temporary bleachers filled with his many friends. Everyone was gazing at her amazing beauty.

He escorted her up a newly reconstructed ramp to stand in front of the bow of his new two hundred and fifty-foot yacht. The hull was of gleaming gold, and it had three stories of pure white super structure. A helicopter sat on a large pod on the roof. Painted in large, white letters on the gold hull were the words *Victory II*. Hanging at the end of a gold ribbon from a high boom was a bottle of the finest California wine from Walter's five hundred-acre vineyard.

Annabelle grasped the bottle and spoke loudly, "I christen thee *Victory II*! May she sail proud throughout the world and be a joy to all who board her with her gallant captain."

Amid shouts from the bleachers of "good luck," Annabelle smashed the bottle against the hull. Then everyone boarded and assembled in the grand lounge on the upper deck and were served a fabulous lunch with a selection of the finest California wines. Then they were taken on a tour of the magnificent vessel.

Annabelle and Walter were sitting close together as he told her that he was leaving Wednesday morning for a short cruise to the Florida Keys. He continued in a quiet word, "I have hired a captain. He and his wife will occupy a bedroom suite. Also a five-star chef and his wife will occupy another bedroom suite. A first mate, two waitresses, two housekeepers, and a mechanic will be quartered below. That leaves ten suite rooms on the first deck, plus a master suite." He looked at her. "How about going with me on this short trip? I must test my crew to determine if they will work together well. We will occupy the master suite together."

Annabelle leaned over and kissed him on the cheek. "After everyone has left, let's try out the bed, and then I'll give you my answer."

Each guest was presented with a miniature shopping cart with a dozen bottles of the finest California wine as they left the vessel.

Chapter 12

Alex Perez was riding home from school on his bike that he built by himself from spare parts he picked up at the local junkyard. He rode past long, low buildings on both side of the road. The road had loading docks and several tractor trailers heavily loaded with produce. He rode past a farm equipment dealership and several farm stands selling fruits and vegetable. He went past a country store and an almost hidden bar and restaurant that catered to farm workers. On the left side of the highway was a two-lane dirt road. A small, hand-painted sign hung from a tree branch, saying "Old Dusty Road."

Alex turned onto the road and rode west for about two miles. There on the right side of the road were long, low warehouse buildings with overhead doors, truck-height loading docks, and then a large, high building that housed farm equipment. Next was a repair shop. Alex rode his bike into the repair shop, parked it, and slid onto a stool in front of a long workbench. Flicking on the overhead fluorescent light, he studied a motor he was building from spare parts to attach a fan to his riding lawn mower.

Across from these buildings, as far as the eye could see, were over one hundred acres of strawberry plants. At the end of the road was a huge expanse of beautiful green lawn, a long line of palm trees on either side, and a tiled walkway edged with beautiful shrubs and flowers that led up to a magnificent Spanish-style hacienda that was two stories high of beige stucco walls, red tiled sloping roofs, and a great oak double front door. A six-foot-high chain link fence surrounded the entire property.

On the west side of the house was a covered walkway, leading to a large patio, an Olympic-sized swimming pool, lounges, chairs, tables with striped umbrellas, and an outdoor bar with a colorful canopy and bright red stools. It was all owned by Maria and Victor Perez and their four children. The oldest son Raymond, now a junior at Florida Atlantic University, was living at home to help as much as possible with the farm work and driving to college in an old Ford that he restored himself. He maintained a steady 4.0 GPA.

Identical twin daughters, Lexi and Ariel, resided together as juniors in the dormitory of the renowned Greenwood Academy for Girls. Both girls were strikingly beautiful with long black eyelashes, dark eyes that sparkled, and shoulder-length curls of jet-black hair. Both were straight-A students. And then there was Alex. Oh, Alex, the true joy of the family. He was perpetual motion, questioning everything and having a passion for anything mechanical. To find Alex when he was not in school, just head to the repair shop. The owners of the junkyard often asked him to find parts for other customers.

His rebuilt thirty-year-old wall phone rang.

"Alex, dinner in thirty minutes."

"Okay, Mom, I'm starved."

Entering the house through the kitchen door at his usual breakneck speed, he saw his parents together in his father's office. Victor was sitting in his leather desk chair; Maria was on the opposite side of the desk on the edge of her seat. The desk was strewn with ledgers and papers. Alex heard whispering. His parents were both leaning very close and speaking Spanish so softly. He could not understand what they were saying. Watching them, he felt sudden uneasiness. His stomach muscles tightened, and he ran to the desk and leaned on the desk with his elbows.

"Mom, Dad, what's wrong?"

His father looked at him with a weak smile and said, "Everything is fine, Alex."

"You're both acting strange," replied Alex. "Just tell me what's wrong."

His mother took his arm as his father said, "I am sure that you know that last year's crop of strawberries suffered because of the drought. So the berries didn't grow large and sweet like they usually do. The same thing is happening again this year. Not enough rain. Our berries aren't growing. We can't afford the cost of an irrigation system for such a large area. We are very concerned that the crop will not mature enough and fail, causing steep financial complications. Please just don't tell your brother or sisters. We'll stay afloat somehow."

The next morning, as Alex was riding his bike to school, he saw a crew of workmen installing TV cables underground at the side of the highway. He stopped to watch. The workers were threading a thick wire cable into a plastic tube, but before inserting the cable into the tube, they were wiping it with thick cotton gloves and then lowering the tube into the trench. He walked his bike over to a worker, obviously the foreman.

"Please tell me, sir. Why are you wiping the cable before you insert it into the plastic tube?"

"Hi ya, kid," he replied and continued to wipe. "As you can see, the cable is very wet, so we have to dry it before putting it in the tube."

"Well, why is it wet?" asked Alex.

"I don't know, kid. All I know is that this special cable draws moisture. Who knows why. Our job is to wipe off the water. We need to change gloves almost every half hour."

"Thank you, mister. That is amazing. How can I get a short piece of the cable?"

"Okay, kid, we unroll it from the huge wooden spindle, and at the end of the day, I'll cut a short piece for you. Come back around four."

"Thanks a lot, mister. I'll be back."

He rode off to school, but his mind was turning so fast that he could not concentrate on his class work. At four o'clock, he spotted the crew several miles from where he first met them.

"Hey, kid, you're just in time. I cut a footlong piece of cable for you."

"Thanks again, mister," replied Alex.

Then pumping the pedals of his bike as fast as he could, he flew into the maintenance shed, put the cable on his workbench, and turned on the overhead light, and he was stunned to see this short piece of cable dripping wet.

Lost in thought, he sat on his stool, examining it as his mind raced. He jumped off the stool, picked up the cable, grabbed a shovel from the wall rack, and ran out of the shop.

From the kitchen, he heard his mother calling, "Alex, are you digging in my vegetable garden?"

"No, Mom, I'm doing an experiment. I won't touch your garden."

He dug a trench the length of the cable and about a foot deep, the same as the work crew had done. Laying the cable into the trench, he covered it up again with the same soil. He ran to his room to his computer to research what type of metal was in the cable.

At dinner, his mother asked, "Why aren't you eating, Alex? You are always starving."

"Sorry, Mom. I'm thinking about an experiment I'm working on."

His father laughed. "Oh, Alex, not another hot idea."

He looked at Raymond sitting opposite him. "Ray, how many feet of string would I need to stretch down each row of our farm?"

Ray also laughed. "Come on, Alex. What kind of question is that?"

Alex smiled. "I'm serious, Ray. I need to know."

"Okay, little brother, I'll ask my computer."

The next morning, even before breakfast, which he never missed, Alex ran out the back door to the garden. Locating the area he buried the cable, he felt the ground, and this small area was wet.

"Dad! Dad! Come here quickly."

"Not now, Alex. I have to start the men on today's work."

"Dad, now, please."

"Okay, Alex, I'm coming."

"Dad, feel the soil here and then the rest of the ground around it."

Victor bent down and sifted some of the damp soil through his fingers. It was wet. He sifted the other soil, and it was bone dry. Alex picked up the shovel that he had left there the night before and dug up the piece of cable.

Victor stood and stared at Alex, who shouted, "I don't know why, but this particular metal draws moisture."

As he ate breakfast, he told his parents the entire story. Victor was not convinced and almost looked annoyed at the delay in starting the day's work.

"Dad, come with me after school, and you will see the cable crew at work. I am trying to tell you that this metal draws moisture for some unknown reason."

They both watched the cable crew wiping the cable dry. Alex took out a pad and copied the name, "Atlas Wire and Cable Company, Philadelphia, PA."

And very excitedly, he shouted, "Come on, Dad. Let's go home. I want to call the company and ask what kind of metal the cable is made of and why it draws moisture."

Alex was able to reach a customer service representative. "Good afternoon. This is the Atlas Wire and Cable Company. How may I direct your call?"

"Yes, thank you," replied Alex. "How can I find out what type of metal is in your TV cable?"

"Sir, we don't reveal our patented process."

"Well then," he asked, "could someone tell me why it draws water?"

"Sir, I am authorized to apologize if you are experiencing some difficulty with our product. We are currently trying to solve this matter and cannot give you an answer at the time. If you leave your name and phone number, we will contact you when we have an answer."

"Thank you. Can you hold for a minute?" asked Alex.

"Dad, let's buy some!" pleaded Alex.

Victor took the phone. "What is the smallest amount we can purchase?"

"Sir, the smallest roll is five hundred feet. The cost is twenty-eight cents a foot, shipped at your expense, and it must be loaded by a regular trucking company with a tailgate. Larger rolls on a wooden spool require a crane to unload. Do you wish to place an order?"

"Thank you. We will call back."

Driving home, Victor said, "Alex, take your sample piece and bury it next to one of the strawberry plants. We'll give it a few days and see the results."

"Great idea, Dad." He then pressed buttons on his cell phone. "Wow, five hundred feet at twenty-eight cents a foot is fourteen thousand dollars. We have to ask Ray to give us the total feet we would need."

"Hold on, Alex," replied Victor. "We aren't there yet."

Three days later, the formerly wilted plant was looking perfect, and the soil around it was damp.

"Hi, Lexi!"

"Hello, Ray. How is my handsome big brother?"

"Seriously, Lexi, can you please come home with Ariel this weekend? Something is going on with Mom and Dad. We have to find out what the problem is."

"Oh, Ray, we'll certainly be home, but can you give us more info?"

"All I know is," Ray replied, "I feel something is wrong."

On Saturday morning, as Mom was standing at the sink, washing the breakfast dishes, the kitchen door opened, and there was Lexi and Ariel. She was so startled that she couldn't speak, only stare.

The twins ran to her kissing and hugging with tears of joy streaming down their cheeks.

"Why are you here?"

Both girls spoke in unison, "Mom, we just need some of your love."

The six of them sat at the kitchen table having lunch and sharing the evident feeling of love.

Victor asked, "So what is the occasion that brings you both here?"

Ray looked at his parents as he spoke, "Dad, Alex has filled us in on the situation. The poor strawberry crops. First of all, we are very upset that you didn't keep us informed. We are family. Alex and I have determined that we will need four rolls of five hundred feet of cable, which totals fifty-six thousand dollars."

Victor interrupted, "Hold on a minute. We have to face the fact that, after two years of failed crops, we don't have fifty-six thousand dollars."

Ray spoke, "Listen, Dad. The four of us have talked this over and decided I will take a leave from college. Lexi and Ariel will transfer from the Greenwood Academy to public school. You can let the field workers go, and we will handle their work."

"No," screamed Maria, starting to tremble with loud sobs.

Victor brushed back his own tears. Trying to control his own emotions, he said quietly but firmly, "Absolutely not. Ray, you are not leaving college." Then he looked at the twins. "You are not leaving the Greenwood Academy. We will raise the money somehow, and we cannot let our Alex down after he has brought us a solution."

There was silence.

"Wait a minute," said Ray. "I have a good friend at school whose mother is a lawyer with the large law firm of Bailey and Forester. Maybe we can get an appointment to discuss our financial needs."

Ariel grinned. "Ray, is this good friend a male or female?"

"None of your business, little sister." He laughed. "I am going into my room and make a phone call."

"Oh yes. In your room." Ariel laughed. "Then it is definitely a female."

They all sat quietly, waiting.

Finally Ray returned. "We have an appointment with John Clark in the Miami office next Monday at ten thirty. I was advised that it will be important for all of us to attend. Is that okay with everyone?"

"Absolutely," replied Victor. "I will gather all our financial information to bring with us."

Chapter 13

O n Monday morning at ten, Victor, Raymond, Lexi, Ariel, and Alex entered the lobby of the Bailey and Forester Law office.

The receptionist asked, "Good morning. May I help you?"

"Yes, please," replied Victor. "We are the Perez family and have an appointment with Mr. John Clark."

She picked up the phone. "Barbara, the Perez family is here for a ten thirty with Mr. Clark. Folks, please take the elevator to the sixth floor. Barbara will meet you."

"Good morning, everyone," Barbara greeted them, smiling and looking at the family standing nervously in front of her at the elevator doors. "Mr. Clark will meet with you in the conference room. Please follow me."

They were just getting seated around a large mahogany table, all looking at the conference room door.

"Good morning, all. I am John Clark. Let's get started. Give me all the pertinent details. Then we will have a discussion."

Mr. Clark listened intently during Victor's presentation and then sat quietly in deep thought. He pressed a button on the intercom. "Barbara, would you please send in Janet with her laptop."

"Yes, sir."

A young man followed with a portable table and chair.

"I am ready, Mr. Clark," he spoke slowly. "I will offer two proposals to the Perez family. Number one is the firm of Bailey and Forester will lend them the money they need to harvest the strawberry crop on their farm. They will pay us one dollar from each box of strawberries sold plus 6 percent interest on the total amount of the loan to be paid at the conclusion of payments. We will take a lien on all farm equipment that will be dismissed when we are paid in full. The one dollar per box will be on the entire crop even if it exceeds the loan amount. The second proposal is the firm of Bailey and Forester will purchase a 20 percent ownership of all crops grown on the present farm. The purchase price will be the amount needed now. The 20 percent ownership will be in perpetuity. I will also inform you as a good faith gesture, if we are to become partners, that a major client of this farm is the United Fruit Company, a worldwide distributor.

"We will check the financial information that you have provided, and if what you provided is true, I will arrange a contract. Also, if you choose option number two, there will be a contract with United to purchase the entire field, providing the quality of the berries are up to their standards. If you choose option number one and agree to the contract with United, you will pay us two dollars additional each box. If you choose option two, please remember we will be partners."

"Mr. Clark," said Victor, "we are most grateful for your proposals. May we have a few moments to discuss this among ourselves?"

"Certainly," he replied. "Notify Barbara when you are ready."

Victor held up his hand. "I believe the second option is in our best interest because being a partner with the Bailey and Forester firm could lead to greater opportunities."

They all agreed.

Victor stated, "Barbara, please inform Mr. Clark that we have reached a decision."

"Mr. Clark, we gratefully accept your second proposal and are ready to proceed."

They all shook hands.

"So partners," Mr. Clark proclaimed, "order the cable and keep me informed of every detail."

———◆———

Just after opening the Palm Beach office on Monday morning, a young man of perhaps seventeen or eighteen years old stumbled into the lobby of the Bailey and Forester Law Firm. He was filthy. His dirty, black hair was matted. His eyes were sunken and darting wildly around. His dirty clothes were torn and covered with grease stains. One shoe was black with mud stuck to it. The other was a worn brown shoe with no socks. He leaned for support against the receptionist desk. The smell was overpowering. The receptionist pressed a button, and immediately two security guards appeared.

They took one look at the bum, and one guard spoke into his shoulder microphone, "Bring two face masks and two pairs of rubber gloves to the main lobby now." Unwilling to touch the young man, the guard said, "Please leave now, and let's not make a problem."

The boy did not move. Only his head turned toward the guards, and in a hoarse whisper, he said, "I am Andrew Vanderbrook the Third."

There was complete silence. Everyone in the lobby turned to stare.

He repeated this time louder, "I am Andrew Vanderbrook the Third."

The guards did not touch him but stood on either side of him.

With great difficulty not to fall and leaning more heavily on the desk, he repeated again, "I am Andrew Vanderbrook the Third."

The receptionist, recovering from the shock of this announcement, pressed a button. "Mr. Rogers, could you please come to the main lobby?"

"Why are you calling me when I am taking depositions?" he yelled as he strolled into the main lobby. He looked angrily at the security guards. "What's your problem? Just throw the bum out." He turned to leave.

Then he heard, "I am Andrew Vanderbrook the Third. I am Annabelle's son."

"What?" shouted Edwin. "What kind of scam is this?"

"This is not a scam," the young man stated. "I am Annabelle's son."

Edwin laughed. "You are crazy or on drugs. Annabelle has no children."

The kid did not flinch or move.

Edwin turned to the guards. "Take him to the locker room, and tell the attendant to put him in the shower and throw away those filthy clothes. I will be there shortly."

Edwin's brain was reeling as he entered the locker room. He called to the attendant, "Hello, Tom. Please call housekeeping after he is cleaned up. Get him some clothes and shoes. Call the kitchen and get him a sandwich. Do not allow him to leave."

Edwin paced his office as he called Annabelle. "Good morning. Vanderbrook residence."

"This is Mr. Rogers. Please tell Miss Vanderbrook that I need to talk to her."

"Mr. Rogers, this is Gretta. Miss Vanderbrook is not here."

"When will she be back?" Edwin asked shortly.

"I don't know, sir. She said she was going on a boat."

"Thank you, Gretta." Then he recalled the event at the boat dock with the new yacht. He pressed a button. "Jane, get me Captain Brad Lacey at Coast Guard Headquarters in Washington, DC"

"Hello, Ed. What can I do for you?" Brad Lacey inquired once he was on the line. "Brad, I need to find Annabelle. She is on a new yacht. I do not know where. It is urgent."

Brad laughed. "Can you give me a little more information?"

"Brad, it's important. All I know is that she christened a new yacht a few days ago in Miami."

"Okay, Ed. Keep calm. I will find her. Should I tell her that you miss her and want her back?"

"Brad, please just find her and tell her that, when I see her, I will give her a swift kick in her beautiful ass."

Edwin then made another call.

"Good morning. Doctor's office."

"Good morning. This is Edwin Rogers. Please tell Dr. Taylor I need to speak with him."

The doctor picked up his line.

"Hi, Doc. Do you have Annabelle's DNA on file?"

"Ed, you know I cannot say anything without her permission."

"Doc, this is very important. Can I send a young man to you for a DNA test to determine if it is a match?"

"Ed, what are you not telling me?"

"Doc, I don't know yet. Please just do this for me, and I need the results ASAP."

Three hours later, Ed got a call back.

"Hello, Ed. It is a match. Annabelle has a son."

Edwin then heard another voice say, "Mr. Rogers, there is an urgent personal call for you on your private line."

Edwin changed phone calls. "Hi, Ed. This is Annabelle. What is the emergency? Three Coast Guard boats are surrounding us."

"What is the emergency?" Ed shouted. "I have your son sleeping on a cot in the office locker room. Damn it, Belle. Talk to me."

There was silence.

"Ed, I will be very grateful if you would take care of him. I will be back as soon as possible and explain. If you have any feeling for me, please do this."

The next morning, every TV station and newspaper on the East Coast had a picture and a story of a dirty, disheveled young man with the headline, "I am Andrew Vanderbrook the Third." The reporters and TV crews were swarming outside the law office, trying to get more information.

<hr>

Several days later, four huge rolls of cable were delivered to the Perez farm. As it was being unloaded, a large van drove in, and twelve men jumped out with shovels, picks, and rakes.

"Mr. Perez, we are here to put the cable in the ground. Mr. Clark sent us."

"Very good," replied Victor. "Dig a trench one foot deep, and lay a cable between two rows of plants all the way to the end."

At twelve o'clock, a truck arrived with lunch for everyone. The men all sat on the grass eating and resting under a large shade tree. *I should go to church this Sunday*, thought Victor, *and pray that Alex is correct.*

The limo stopped in front of the twenty-story high-rise apartment building. Annabelle hurried out of the car, ran into the lobby, moved past the receptionist, and entered the elevator, punching in the code that took her directly to the twentieth-floor penthouse apartment of Edwin Rogers.

Emerging directly into the foyer of his apartments, Edwin was waiting for her. She ran into his outstretched arms, circled his neck, and kissed him. As her body pressed against his, he felt something stirring in his crotch, and she felt it also and whispered, "Later. Where is he?"

"Your son is in my guest room. He has been sleeping and eating for three days except for when he is in the shower."

Annabelle quickly pushed open the bedroom door. Andrew was sitting on the edge of the bed, holding his stomach. He was looking a lot better than when she had last seen him in the park.

She sat on the bed next to him, took his hands, and said quietly, "You can get through this. I am here to help you."

Andrew looked at her without a reply but placed his hand over hers and rocked back and forth.

Edwin walked in. "Belle, I need answers. Who is the father?"

Annabelle raised her head, looked at him, and mumbled, "Please, Ed, I cannot talk about it now. Trust me."

She also realized that he was very confused. His mind was racing. How could this happen to a girl that grew up with every luxury possible, went to the best schools, and was a member of a privileged society? Did she have an affair?

He was the attorney for the entire family. He knew every detail of her life as well as the families. Ultra-wealthy lifestyles always protected with heavy security.

"How could this happen?"

Victor walked through the rows of strawberry plants. He could not believe what he was seeing, bright red berries, three times larger than any he had ever seen.

He picked three beautiful ripe berries and went into the kitchen. "Maria! Come look at these berries. They're all ripe and ready to be picked."

He put them on a dish and cut one in half. He handed it to Maria, and they took a bite and looked at each other. The berries were as sweet as candy.

Just then the phone rang.

"Good morning, Mr. Perez. This is John Clark. Are you ready for picking?"

"Yes," Victor replied, "the berries are beautiful."

Early the next morning, a bus arrived on the farm with twenty men. A foreman handed each man a large shoulder bag.

"Let's get to work!" he ordered.

For five days, tractor trailers were backed up to the loading docks. On the side of each cab was lettered "United Fruit Distributors."

At the law office, a phone was ringing. "Good morning, Bailey and Forester Law Office. How may I help you?"

"Yes, please. This is Mike from the United Fruit Distribution Company. May I speak with John Clark?" He waited for the transfer. "Hello, John! I have never seen strawberries so large and beautiful. I downloaded the price and sold the entire crop to a national chain. The VP called and told me they were selling them by the pound instead of by the box. John, I want a contract now for the next crop."

"That's great, Mike," said John. "Now listen to me carefully. I am sure there will be a frenzy of agriculture experts banging down the door, dying to know the origin of the berries and the location of where you purchased them. Please reply and mark the crates 'Grown in USA.' Please do not give out any more information."

"Absolutely, John. Just send me the new contracts, okay?"

<hr/>

Edwin took Annabelle's hand and led her into his bedroom. She stood still as he undressed her. They made tender, emotional love, not erotic. Just pure and sweet love. They climaxed together and, with complete satisfaction, stayed in bed, side-by-side.

Edwin, leaning on one elbow facing her, said softly, "Sweetheart, we will get through this together. We will see that Andrew stays clean. We will hire a tutor to determine his grade level. Give a large donation to the Greenwood

Academy for Boys and forget the past. You know, Belle, he is tall and handsome. He looks a lot like your father."

Then a horrible thought raced through his mind. His body gave a shudder and became tense. Annabelle raised his arm and jumped out of bed. Their eyes met. In that moment, the unspeakable truth hit him like a ton of bricks. Her father had raped her.

Randolph Forester and Thomas Bailey sat across from each other at a long conference table in their office in Atlanta. After a long silence, they both blurted out at once, "This is crazy!"

"You're right, Tom," said Randy. "We need to get back to work!"

"Enough sitting around, drinking too much coffee, and reading about others' successes in business journals. Our wives are completely consumed with the law offices. We have the money. We have the time. Let's create something again."

"Right on, cousin," replied Randy. "Let's hop down to Palm Beach and look around." Randy made a call. "Good morning, Sam. This is Randy. I want you to warm up the chopper. We're going for a little ride."

"Sounds great, boss," he answered. "I was wondering how long it would be before you guys got moving again."

A bit later, they cruised around flying low.

"Sam, make a few passes over Okeechobee Boulevard and give us a look at the City Place area."

"What are we looking for, boss?" Sam asked.

"We don't know," they both replied.

"Okay, boss, how about the Palm Beach Lakes area? I used to pilot a private jet for a couple that lived there."

"Okay, Sam, put us down in that parking lot."

Just then a taxicab came alongside the chopper.

"Hey, mister, do you need a ride?" asked the driver.

"Of course," replied Randy. Turning to Sam, Randy requested he wait for them.

After about thirty minutes of driving around, the driver asked, "What are you guys looking for?"

"We aren't really sure," replied Randy. "How about taking us to a good place for lunch?"

"I don't really know what to recommend, to be honest. You fellas look pretty rich."

"Take us to a fast-food drive-in. We'll pick up sandwiches and head back to the chopper."

Randy spoke to Tom, "A lot of people must be living in this area. Where do they dine?"

The three of them sat in the chopper, eating sandwiches. Both Randy and Tom were lost in thought.

"Tom, let's build a very different, very expensive, one-of-a-kind restaurant."

"That's a capital idea," replied Tom.

Back at the office, Randy said, "Lois, get me Walter MacCormant on the phone."

The firm of MacCormant and Littleton was a recognized leading architectural firm, specializing in designing beautiful, unique buildings. "Lois, also get me Debbie Winger at the Winger Real Estate brokerage company."

"Yes, sir," she replied.

The business world was well aware of the reputation of the Forester and Bailey families' huge successes and the amassing of great wealth. In an hour, seated at the conference table were Walter MacCormant and Debbie Winger.

"Thank you both for being here on such short notice," said Tom. "Randy and I want to build and create the most elegant and most expensive restaurant in South Florida, and we don't care what it costs. Debbie, I need you to find us a great location with plenty of parking and easy access from the Palm Beach International Airport. Walter, get your team to dream up a building that has never been built before."

Debbie and Walter began asking questions. Randy held up his hand in the time-out signal.

"Listen carefully," he continued. "You guys are the professionals. You tell us, but dream big and lavish."

For the next three days, they were in front of the computers, researching and gathering information, making notes about great restaurants throughout the world.

"Good morning, gentlemen," Lois called on the intercom. "Debbie Winger on line one."

"Thank you, Lois, and a good morning to you also." They picked up the line. "Debbie! Do you have good news?"

"Yes, Randy, I need to call a meeting. I can be there in a half hour. Call Walter also."

As they got off the phone, Randy pressed the intercom button and asked Lois to join them in the meeting with a laptop to record the conversation.

A bit later, Debbie opened her briefcase. She took out lots of pictures—area and land photos, area maps, and over a hundred miscellaneous photos. They spent some time studying the material.

Then Debbie spoke, "What we have here is a very old building in the final stages of collapsing. It's well over sixty years old. Originally it was a three-story hotel. It has been abandoned for at least forty years and has been declared unsafe by the local building inspectors. The building itself is three hundred feet wide and four hundred feet deep. It's decayed and falling apart. The roof has fallen in. It should really be demolished. As you can see in the pictures, there is no glass in the rotted window frames, and the old shutters are hanging in every direction. But here is the good news, gentlemen. This hotel is the best location in Palm Beach. This land area is over ten acres with great access from Palm Beach Lakes Boulevard and is very close to the Palm Beach International Airport. I have spent an entire day in the county clerk's office, trying to track down the owners. Finally I have discovered that this property was left in a will to a woman that lives in London. Her name is Margaret Wilder, and apparently she is the heir to a vast real estate empire throughout Europe and owns this property. I was surprised to see that the real estate taxes have been paid on time all these years by a solicitor in England. I have doubts that she even knows about this property."

Randy jumped up. "Holy mackerel! Margaret Wilder's son, Jason, is married to Tom's sister, Alexis." Randy instantly picked up the white phone and pressed only one button.

"What's up, Randy?"

As he glanced at the others in the room and winked at Tom, he said "Sandy, if you don't come home early tonight, I'll come to your office and show you what's up."

Everyone tried to hide his or her embarrassment at this. Sandy was silent.

Then she spoke, "Randy honey, I promise I'll be home for dinner, but why did you call me?"

"I need some free legal work."

Sandy laughed. "So find yourself a lawyer. I am too busy."

Not showing the least embarrassment, he said, "Okay, everyone, my wife is going to handle this."

"Good work, Debbie! I thank you all for being here. Let's all meet again Monday morning. Walter, take these plans and photos and get some ideas. If possible, I want sketches too. I'm confident that we'll work it out with Mrs. Wilder."

When Sandy arrived home, he was already in the hot tub. She quickly undressed and slipped in beside him, and they embraced each other. Not speaking, she straddled him, and they had ridiculously frantic sex. It was quickly over, and neither spoke or looked at each other.

"Honey," said Sandy quietly, "we're both too deeply in love for this, and I know it is my fault."

"So sweetheart," Randy answered, "I have to be in Palm Beach for a few days to look at a property. Please come with me. We can check into the Breakers and be alone for a couple days."

With tears welling up in her eyes, she kissed him and replied, "Yes, yes."

They arrived at the hotel in the late afternoon.

"Good afternoon, Mr. and Mrs. Forester. Welcome to the Breakers. If there is anything I can do for you, please don't hesitate to call me. My name is Aldo."

"Yes," answered Randy, "please secure us a reservation for tonight in a center booth at the Green Tequila."

Sandy chimed in, "For eight o'clock please."

"Oh boy!" Aldo chuckled. "Friday night, three hours away, and center booth? That won't be cheap, Mr. Forester."

Randy shook hands with him and handed him a crisp bill. "Just make it happen."

In the elevator, he turned to Sandy. "Isn't eight o'clock a little late for dinner?"

"It is," replied Sandy, "but you're going to make passionate love to me first."

The Green Tequila was packed with beautiful people, both men and women, wearing the latest fashions of dresses, and many girls were in various states of undress. At the long bar, every seat was taken, and row after row of young people were standing, talking, laughing, drinking, and checking out the possibilities for later.

As they slid into a center booth, a waiter in a tuxedo appeared. "May I take your drink orders?"

"Yes, two green tequilas with a plate of crackers and an assortment of cheese."

They touched glasses, and their eyes met and sparkled. They both realized silently how wonderful it was to be in love.

The maître d' approached. "Excuse me. There is a couple at the door. They claim they are acquainted with you and would like to join you."

Randy started to shake his head in refusal, but Sandy exclaimed, "It's Jason and Alexis!"

Waving them over, Randy slid over to one side next to Sandy. Jason and Alexis moved into the booth and sat across. Reaching over with a long kiss, Sandy greeted Alexis. Then it was warm handshakes for the men.

Sandy was so excited to see Alexis. She shouted, "This is fabulous. What are you doing here in America? When did you arrive? Where are you staying?"

"Time out." Jason laughed. "First of all, what type of place is this? It cost me a bloody fortune just to get in the door."

"Jason darling, please change seats with me. I need to sit next to Sandy."

The two girls were practically sitting on top of each other and talking and laughing so intensely. They held each other and didn't even look back at their husbands.

Randy didn't hesitate to relate the details of the property to Jason. He listened silently and replied, "Dear brother-in-law, let us meet tomorrow and talk business. Tonight is for fun."

Turning to the girls, Jason said loudly to interrupt them, "Ladies, this is a great restaurant. I'm also having a great deal of difficulties in keeping my eyes off the half-naked women. So tonight, let's eat, drink, and laugh. Randy and I will show you both how suave and debonair we are in the hopes of getting laid later."

They all exploded with laughter. Alexis looked at them with great difficulty in trying not to laugh.

"You guys are going to have to do a lot better than that for us to be willing victims of your lust."

Randy, never to be shy when he sensed something interesting, asked, "Jason, why are you here?"

"Tomorrow, dear Randy."

"Hello, Tom. Sorry to call you so late. Listen, Jason and Alexis are here. Ask Dahlia, and tell her it's important. And you both fly here to the Breakers as early in the morning as possible."

Tom and Randy were just finishing breakfast.

"So now," shouted Jason as he strode into the dining room and shook hands with Tom, "what are you two blokes up to?"

"Would you like some breakfast?" asked Randy.

"No, sir, I had breakfast in bed after a wonderful repeat of last night's action."

"Good," replied Randy. "We have a limo waiting. We want to show you a property owned by your mother."

"Hold on. My mother doesn't own any property in Florida. I would know because I'm in complete charge of all her holdings."

Randy handed him a thick folder. "Let's go. We'll show you everything as we drive."

Jason was engrossed in reading the material furnished by Debbie. Tom looked silently at Randy and shook his head, indicating Jason as they realized the complete transformation in his attitude. Jason's eyes were narrow. He studied the information slowly.

He called the driver, "My good man, make a right at the next intersection. Then drive two and a half miles, and turn left on to Legend Drive. Go down four miles and turn left again. And then go two and a half miles and then another left back here."

As the hotel came into view, Jason leaned forward. "Driver, please stop. Can you circle that old building?"

"I'm sorry, sir," replied the driver. "It's too overgrown, and there are deep potholes."

Jason stepped out. "Be a good fellow, and wait here."

He slowly walked around the building and then stood in the middle of the overgrown parking lot.

"I smell trouble," whispered Tom.

Jason reentered the car. "Please take us back to the hotel, driver."

They sat in a secluded corner of the lobby.

He said, "I must make Mother aware of this property; however, I can assure you I am in charge." When no one spoke, he continued, "Please reveal your plan."

Randy could not believe he was allowing himself to be intimidated. "We plan to turn the old hotel into the finest restaurant in South Florida. The land surrounding it is needed for parking."

He gave a quick look at Tom. They understood each other perfectly that he didn't want it to sound too grand. They waited.

Without a smile, Jason answered, "Okay, here's the deal. This is a take-it-or-leave-it offer. We form a limited liability partnership. I put up the property for a 10 percent ownership in the entire project. You blokes are responsible for everything to complete this plan. Also it is now eleven o'clock. You have one hour to agree, or the offer is off the table. I want to thank you both for bringing this valuable property to my attention." He got up and walked away without another word.

They looked at each other in shock.

Then Randy said, "Tom, can you believe this? He sounds like us, but I believe we've met our match. We have to discuss this with the girls, and I'm talking about some serious money, Tom."

After a few minutes, the three girls walked in, arm in arm, laughing. "What do you boys want? We weren't finished in the spa."

Randy gave them all the details and conversation with Jason.

Alexis interrupted, "Would you rather I left?"

"No!" they all shouted.

Randy began again, and Alexis interrupted him again. She began slowly and softly she said, "That's my Jason," looking at Sandy and Dahlia.

"Now that you have the details, what's the opinion of the two greatest legal minds of America?" Randy asked.

Alexis interrupted again, "Everyone listen to me. Jason has a business mind like a steel trap. He has proven over and over that he is brilliant in business decisions. He would not have offered the property unless he knows it will be a good deal. I can also guarantee, knowing my Jason, he will not hesitate to do the project himself. That's the way he is. Business is business to him, and the amount of money you figured it would take is pocket change to the Wilder family."

Sandy and Dahlia stood up. "Guys, you have your answer, and remember it is a limited liability agreement. Dahlia and I will prepare all the legal documents, so go for it. Come on, Alexis. A massage is waiting."

The notices were posted on both bulletin boards.

"On Saturday night, a dance social will be held for girls and boys who are students of Greenwood Academy. There will be a twelve-piece band and refreshments. It will be held at 7:00 p.m. in the girls' school gymnasium, there will be no additional guests, and both school principals will chaperon. Dress is neat casual."

A group of boys, including Andrew, was standing around with loud, forced laughter and nervously scanning all of the girls. Against the opposite wall was a group of girls talking and trying not to be too evident as they looked at the boys.

Andrew saw this tall, slim girl with jet-black hair that cascaded with curls to her shoulders. He stood still and stared at her. Just then she looked up and realized that this boy was looking at her. She smiled and resumed the conversation with the others. Andrew couldn't take his eyes off her. She was stunning.

With an air of confidence, he sauntered over to her. "Would you care to dance with me?"

She looked at him, smiled, and replied with a vibrant, "Yes!"

He took her hand, led her on to the dance floor, circled her waist with his right arm, and then held her left hand very lightly. The band was playing the fox-trot. With his three months of dance lessons that his mother insisted on paying for, Andrew knew just how to hold her gently but firmly. Smoothly and effortlessly, he led her around the dance floor. She was amazed how he moved her with the music. When the song ended, he continued to hold her.

"My name is Andrew. My friends call me Andy."

She smiled. "My name is Lexi. My friends call me Lexi." And she laughed.

Still holding her hand, he walked with her to the bandleader. She looked at him as he whispered. The band began to play the beautiful Blue Danube waltz that he had requested.

He again circled her waist, took her hand, and, with perfect timing, whirled and swayed as they moved beautifully with the waltz. She could not believe how easily and tenderly he held her. They flowed with the music. She was not sure if her shoes even touched the floor, and almost too suddenly, it ended.

"Would you like any refreshments?" he asked.

"Sure," she replied, still holding his hand they walked to the table.

She sat looking at him. He brought two glasses of punch and a plate of fancy cakes. In his shirt pocket were napkins. They sat quietly eating and drinking. They started to talk at the same time and laughed.

"What is your last name?" he inquired.

"My name is Lexi Perez," she replied.

She immediately saw the look in his eyes and the lines on his forehead. She stood up while looking him in the eyes, and without a smile, she said, "Andrew, thank you for asking me to dance."

And she walked away without looking back. Andrew sat very still as he realized what just happened. That night, he couldn't sleep. He tossed and turned as he thought about her and how much of a jerk he was. *So her name is Perez. So what? That's not the person I am.*

He got out of bed, dressed, and decided, since it was Sunday, he would take a drive back home to see his mother and clear his mind. On Sunday, all the household staff was off. He and Annabelle were at the kitchen table eating pizza.

With hesitation, he began, "Mother, I met this girl last night, and I can't get her off my mind. Her beauty, the way she walks, talks, and her smile."

Annabelle looked at him. "That's wonderful, Andrew. I am happy to hear this. What is her name? Maybe I know her family. Is she a student at Greenwood?"

"Her name is Lexi Perez."

Annabelle jumped and shouted, "Did you say Perez?"

He stood up, put on his jacket, went to his mother, kissed her on the cheek, and left her with, "I have to get back to school."

The next afternoon, he was outside the fence of the girls' school.

A security guard approached him. "Can I help you?"

"Yeah, I want to find a girl I met at the dance on Saturday night."

"I'm sorry. You have to leave."

Not moving, he saw a group of girls standing on the lawn. He followed the fence to get closer, and then he saw her.

"Lexi!" he yelled. "Lexi! Lexi!"

But no girl turned to him.

He yelled again even louder, "Lexi!"

One girl looked at him. He saw her.

"Lexi, please just talk to me," he pleaded.

She walked to the fence. "I'm not Lexi. I'm Ariel. We're identical twins. You must be Andrew. Didn't you hurt her enough? She's in our dorm in a deep funk. Please get back in your fancy convertible and go away. Leave her alone."

"No, Ariel," he blurted out. "I have to see her. Please tell her." He drove away.

———————◆———————

"Good afternoon, Miss Vanderbrook. I am Mrs. Johnson, principal of the Greenwood Academy for Boys. Is Andrew home? He didn't sleep in his dorm room last night, and he didn't attend any of his classes today."

"Thank you for calling, Mrs. Johnson. Andrew wasn't feeling well last night so he drove home."

Annabelle's mind was racing. *It's that girl*, she thought. *Maybe Andrew was with her.* She wondered how she could find him though. She called Edwin.

"What's the matter, Belle? It's ten o'clock," asked Edwin.

"Ed, please, I need you. Andrew isn't in school, and I haven't heard from him."

"Take it easy," he replied. "I'll be right over."

He opened her front door with his key and called out to her.

She ran into his arms. "Ed, what do we do?"

"Belle, calm down. Get your coat. My car is out front. Tell me what happened as we drive."

In the car, she told him about the Perez girl and her reaction.

She looked at him. "Where are we going?" He gave her hand a reassuring pat. He parked the car near the entrance of the downtown park.

"Hold my arm," he instructed.

As they walked, he searched. His eyes scanned past all of the less fortunate homeless people. Suddenly he pointed to a bench where Andrew was sitting peculiarly with his head straight forward.

They ran over to him. His lips were moving, and he kept repeating over and over again, "Yes, Mother dear, her name is Lexi Perez."

Ed took his arm and lifted him up gently. "Come on, Andrew. We're going home."

In the car as they drove home, Edwin asked Andrew if he were all right. "Are you high?"

"No," replied Andrew.

Eating breakfast in the morning, Annabelle sat next to him. "You're my son. You're very dear to me, and I'm glad you're okay. I'm so sorry that I spoke without thinking. I was temporarily blinded by the importance of social status that has been an important part of my life."

"Please contact Ms. Perez and invite her to lunch on Saturday so I can meet her. I want to see her because your happiness is my priority."

"Thank you, Mother. I really appreciate that, and when you meet Lexi, you'll see why I'm infatuated. I also want very much to please you and to be a worthy son of our name and reputation. I promise to never hurt you again."

<hr />

"Lexi, it's Andrew. Please don't hang up."

"Why are you calling me? How did you get my number?"

"Lexi, please just give me a minute. My mother's friend is a lawyer. I begged him to get me your number. I want to invite you to a lunch on Saturday at my home to meet my mother. Please say yes."

There was silence.

"Andrew, hold on."

"Hello? This is Lexi's mother. How about we invite you over to our home on Saturday so we can meet you?"

"Yes, ma'am. What time?" he quickly replied.

"Let's try for one o'clock."

On Friday night, there was no chance of sleeping. On Saturday morning, he was a nervous wreck, trying on every article of clothing he had, trying to find the perfect fit. Annabelle knocked on his door and entered his room. She noticed all the clothes on his bed and chair and the shoes scattered on the floor.

"Andrew honey, I know what you're going through. Don't be nervous though. You just have to be yourself, and you'll be fine. Here, wear these slacks, this shirt, this white pullover, and these shoes with no socks."

He made it over to the Perez house, and Lexi met him at the large oak front door.

"Hi, Lexi! Thank you for inviting me." He handed her a box of beautifully wrapped chocolates.

She smiled. "Welcome. Just remember to look at the L on my shirt. Ariel's has an A. Please come in."

Maria walked over. "Hello, I'm Mrs. Perez. Welcome to our home. We're sitting down for lunch in the kitchen."

He followed them. He looked at Lexi, and he felt his knees turn to rubber. He couldn't breathe. He heard a voice behind him. It was Ariel.

She whispered to her mother, "This boy looks like trouble."

Lexi didn't move either.

Ray stood. "I'm Raymond. You already met Ariel, who is trying to hide the box of chocolates. That's our little brother Alex. Our father will be here in a few minutes. Please sit here next to Lexi."

Andrew was obviously incredibly nervous and sat without speaking. Everyone was staring at him. He was tall and very handsome with broad shoulders. He had sparkling hazel eyes and a head full of sandy-colored hair.

Victor called out, "Where is everybody?"

"We're all in the kitchen," replied Ariel.

Victor strode in and looked at everyone. "Why the long faces? Did somebody die?" He looked over and saw Andrew. He leaned over. "You'll be all right, son." And he laughed.

He took his place at the head of the table with a huge grin. Soon enough they were talking, laughing, and telling stories of school life and farm activities.

Andrew overcame his nervousness and entered the conversations. He told humorous anecdotes about life in the boy's dorm. The only one sitting quietly was Lexi. Without thinking, Andrew was holding her hand. Even when gesturing and talking, he wouldn't let go. Marie did not miss that.

Suddenly Victor stood up. "Oh, gosh. Would you all believe that it's already four o'clock? Come on, Alex. Let's go put away the mowers." He looked at Andrew. "It was our pleasure that you had lunch with us today!"

Andrew also stood, still holding Lexi's hand. "Mr. Perez, this has been a wonderful experience for me! It must feel great to be a part of such a loving family. Thank you all for inviting me. Lexi, would you walk with me to my car?"

"I guess I have to since you're still holding my hand," she replied

As Andrew drove away waving, Ray asked, "So what do you think, Mom?"

She replied, "I think he's a nice boy, but it was strange that, with all the conversations, he never mentioned anything about his family. Never spoke of his parents. Never once even alluded to his family's immense wealth or way of life as a rich young man. No stories of his childhood, but he was certainly impressive."

"Mom, as he was leaving, I heard him tell Lexi that he wanted to be with her. Lexi told him that she wanted to be with him too, but it wouldn't work. They just live in different worlds. He didn't even answer her. He just kissed her and drove away."

Sitting at their desk in their dorm, Andrew and his best friend and roommate, Leon Delesante, were engrossed with their homework.

"Hey, bro," Leon asked. "It just occurred to me that we don't argue politics anymore. We don't talk sports. All I hear from you is about the Perez girl. After hearing so much about her, I would be a better fit than you. Vanderbrook and Perez? No way, man. Why don't you introduce me to her and see what happens?"

"Oh, sure," replied Andrew. "You have zero chance of that happening, but she does have a twin sister."

"Really?" Leon shouted, laughing. "If what you're saying is true, how about introducing me?"

"I don't know, Leon. Even though we're best friends, I might take a big risk of losing Lexi because of your good looks and smooth-talking sensibilities."

"Come on, Andrew. I would never do that to you. I wouldn't risk our friendship like that. I value our friendship above all. Why don't you just set up a double date?"

Andrew called the Perez house. "Hello, Mrs. Perez. This is Andrew."

"Hello, Andrew. How are you?"

"I'm fine, thank you. Could you put Ariel on the phone?"

"You mean Lexi, don't you?"

"No, ma'am. I would like to speak to Ariel."

"Okay, I'll go get her."

"Ariel, listen to me please. I would very much like to introduce my best friend and roommate to you. His name is Leon Delasante. His father is Marco Delasante, the state senator from Miami. I have to warn you ahead of time that he is very ugly and doesn't have any manners, but he's my best friend."

Ariel laughed. "Why would I want to meet anyone that's ugly and doesn't have any manners?"

"Because I told him the same about you."

"Hold on, Andrew."

"Hello? This is Mrs. Perez."

"I know, Mrs. Perez. I can assure you that I take this request very seriously. Leon is my best friend and a gentleman. I would not be asking if I thought there were any risk."

"We'll call you back in a few minutes."

"Hi, Lexi." As she answered the phone, he could feel his entire body tingle to the sound of her voice.

"What's this all about, Andrew?"

"Sweetheart," he replied. He stopped when he realized what he just said.

Lexi was silent and then whispered, "Are you sure?"

"Are you asking me if I am sure that you're a sweetheart or if I'm sure about a double date with Leon?"

"Both," replied Lexi. "We'll meet you."

"Great, we will pick you up Sunday at noon. I will make lunch reservations at the Breakers Hotel in Palm Beach."

"Wait a minute, Andrew."

He heard muffled voices.

"We will meet you there at one o'clock. Ariel would feel more comfortable if we drove our own car. Is that okay?"

"You bet it is, Lexi, and tell Ray he doesn't have to follow you. Your safety is guaranteed."

The minute that Leon touched Ariel's hand in greeting, their eyes met, and they both knew that their lives had changed forever.

On Monday morning, three double-wide trailers were delivered on the site of the old hotel. A food catering truck was installing a fifty-foot-long by twenty-five-foot-wide tent. Inside were long tables and chairs to feed the workers. Two cranes were extended high above the roofline. High low tractors with working platforms were lined up. Walter MacCormant arrived with six men, all carrying rolls of blueprints. Inside one of the trailers, they unrolled the blueprints on one of the long tables.

Except for Walter, they all wore different color hard hats that identified the different trades they were responsible for. Randy and Tom arrived. Walter called for attention, speaking slowly but firmly looking at all the men.

"Each one of you will receive copies of the entire project. It is your responsibility to coordinate every detail. This is a very complicated and unique design. Never been done before. So work together and ask questions if you aren't absolutely sure of something. We are not changing the exterior front only. We will secure everything the way it looks now. That will be the look of the front when the building is completed. The broken windows, crooked shutters, old siding, and peeling paint will all be secured and remain except for a new roof and giant steel beams to support it. The ground floor will be completely opened up to the three-story-high ceiling. All the interior corners will be rounded, and the two upper floors on three sides of the interior balconies will be installed on the back and the two sides. They will jut out twenty-five feet deep, wrap around the walls, and open into the center courtyard area. When this phase is completed, you will receive the finishing plans. There will be a progress report meeting every day at 6:30 a.m."

"Tom, I have the perfect name for our restaurant. Let's call it the Shack. From the exterior entryway, it would look like an abandoned shack, but once you get inside, it would be absolutely breathtaking."

"That's a great idea, Randy. The plan that Walter and his team dreamed up was brilliant, but it will cost millions. I think we need our own project manager."

"Paula!" they both blurted out together, startling Walter. "Paula is a trusted associate and an extremely capable manager."

"Believe us, Walter. You would be very glad to have her." Randy took out his cell phone. "Lois, find Paula and have her call us on my cell phone."

Ten minutes later, Randy's phone rang. "Hi, boss. What a pleasure to hear from you."

"Paula, I'm putting you on speaker, and stop calling me boss."

Tom asked, "What are you doing?"

She replied, "With your help, we are now in great shape financially. My husband also retired. And would you believe that he is enrolled in a culinary school just to keep busy? I have never washed so many pots and dishes. I'm going nuts."

"Okay, Paula. You and Jack are moving back to Palm Beach. We need you to be a project manager on a new building we are involved with."

They gave her all the details.

Paula was silent the entire time and listened intently. "Okay, guys. Tell Sam to pick us up with the chopper next Monday morning. Thank you guys so much. You both just saved our marriage and my sanity. But enough hugging and kissing. What's our salary?"

Randy and Tom looked at each other without a smile. "Who said anything about a salary?"

They hung up and started laughing.

"What's that all about?" demanded Jack.

"Don't worry, honey. We won't be able to spend all the money they will deposit in our bank account."

The next four months were a blur. Paula was racing around in her golf cart, studying the blueprints and checking every detail, constantly on her cell phone while talking to Randy and Tom. She was conversing with Walter or the six other men. Meanwhile Jack was in a trailer office, doing all the purchasing, checking every invoice, calling for price quotes, watching the truck deliveries, supervising six office workers, paying bills, handling payroll details with time clocks, and doing everything else under the sun.

Alexis pulled into the massive parking lot in her Rolls-Royce. Every space had a letter and a number painted on it. A golf cart with a security sign on the roof approached.

"Excuse me," she asked. "Is this Palm Beach Lakes Boulevard?"

"Yes, ma'am, it is," replied the security worker. "I'm looking for the new restaurant that is being built."

"Well, this is it, ma'am." He held up a walkie-talkie. "Harley section one."

Another security golf cart drove up. "Good morning, ma'am. Please follow me."

Alexis then saw the building. She pressed the horn, and everybody stopped what they were doing. "This must be a mistake. This is some old, broken-down shack."

"Yes, ma'am. That's the restaurant. We will have to enter through the kitchen as the front doors are locked. Please park next to that Mercedes."

At the kitchen door, another guard asked for Alexis' ID.

"I'm here to see Paula. I am Mrs. Wilder."

On the walkie-talkie, the guard said, "Paula, there's a Mrs. Wilder to see you."

"Thank you. Show her in, please. I'll be there in a minute."

"Good morning, Mrs. Wilder. I'm Paula."

"I can't believe I'm finally meeting you. You're really famous. Call me Alexis."

"Hop into my golf cart, and I'll give you a grand tour."

Alexis was speechless, seeing a four hundred-foot-long and three hundred-foot-wide open courtyard. The two balconies were constructed with a clear view of the main floor. A three-story-high ceiling was completely mirrored.

Alexis said, "Paula, I am designing the interior décor. I need an assistant. This is beyond believable."

"Well, Alexis, I have assigned two secretaries that are in the main office. You just speak into this mic, and they will record your every word. Let's take this elevator up to the top where I have my private two-seat gondola that travels along the ceiling so you can get a better look. As you see, we have four elevators with clear glass windows on three sides so you can see all the action. Each balcony wraps around the dining room on each floor. We will have a moving walkway that can take you with a maître d' to your table.

Seated in the gondola, they rode throughout the building.

Alexis said, "Paula, I have traveled the world, and I have been to many famous restaurants, but I have never seen anything this breathtaking."

Paula smiled. "What do you think about a pure, all-white decor?"

"Well," replied Alexis, "I have samples of many beautiful colors because, quite frankly, white is boring."

"Okay, I have a golf cart and a driver waiting for you. If there is anything you need or care for, just ask. Speak into the mic to record your thoughts."

Alexis took out her cell. "Hi, Jason. You would not believe how magnificent this restaurant is. It's beyond anything we have ever seen. I just wanted to tell you that I love you, honey. I have to get back to work. Good-bye, babe."

"Are you ready, ladies? Here are my instructions. We will use five different shades of lavender. I will leave the samples. Walls will be pale lavender. All trim will be two shades darker than the walls. There will be crown molding on the balcony dining area and courtyard area. Twelve inches below are to be the ceiling fixtures, which are to be two shades darker than the trim. Also there will be hanging ceiling fixtures. Floors are to be skidproof. Italian marble will be the same color as the walls. I also need fluorescent lavender lighting on the railings of the balcony. The dance floor is to be twelve-inch-wide wood boards with thin tubes of lighting between each board, also lavender color. Fluorescent lights will be on the edges of all balcony edges. Wall light fixtures will be on the balcony at every ten feet, all lavender. Please give everyone involved a copy."

"Walter, have you seen Paula? I wanted to say good-bye," said Alexis.

"She is on the roof, supervising the installation of the chopper landing pad."

A few months later, everything was ready for the grand opening. A sign went up inside the front door, "Occupancy limit: 1200." The celebration had to be a two-night affair. The first night was families, close friends, and important people involved in the construction. It was really a test for the next night when the rich and powerful of the country were invited.

On the second night, the media trucks were already lining up at the entrance. All four hundred employees were well trained and in place. The breathless amazement of the guests as they entered was beyond belief. The place was straight out of a dream. It was paradise. With the exquisite furnishing and the vivid colors, everything was perfect. The dance floor was packed. The world-famous Lavender Girls dance band with maestro Lisa Harper and her magical clarinet thrilled the dancers as they held the one they loved and swayed with the enchanting music. Every seat at every table was taken. The balcony dining was a favorite. To be able to watch the action below was amazing. The grandeur and opulence was beyond anyone's imagination.

A voice over the intercom announced, "Vanderbrook, party of four, your table is ready."

Sandy's parents, Byron, and Dina came forward. So did Annabelle and Edwin. Then came Andrew with Lexi. The maître d' was puzzled, and so were the eight people standing at the rope.

"Ladies and gentlemen, I do have a table for eight on the upper balcony. It is a great location. We only have one table for four available, and the next one may not be available for an hour. Perhaps you would agree to this."

Both Charles and Annabelle agreed. But Lexi was petrified. She had never experienced such opulence.

Andrew squeezed her hand and whispered, "Lexi, you look really beautiful. Just be yourself and stay close to me, okay?"

The waiter approached. "May I have your drink orders?"

Edwin said, "Can you serve a green tequila?"

"Yes, sir."

Edwin continued, "Folks, it is a great drink. Why don't you try it?"

They all agreed.

The waiter looked at Andrew and Lexi. "May I please see an ID?"

Andrew smiled. "We will each have an Arnold Palmer. Thank you, sir."

Dina asked, "What is an Arnold Palmer?"

Andrew replied, "It is sweet tea mixed with lemonade."

Charles spoke up, "Let us all introduce ourselves. I am Charles Vanderbrook."

"I am Carol Vanderbrook, his wife."

"I am Byron Vanderbrook."

"I am Dina Vanderbrook, his wife."

"I am Annabelle Vanderbrook."

"I am Edwin Rogers, managing partner of the law firm of Bailey and Forester."

"I am Andrew Vanderbrook, Annabelle's son." Then he realized that Lexi could not speak. She was so nervous. Andrew continued, "This is my beautiful Lexi Perez."

Charles looked at him and repeated, "Andrew, Andrew. I had a brother Andrew. He was killed in a plane crash."

Edwin said quietly, "He was Annabelle's father." He took her hand and squeezed.

Everyone was silent. Then the questions started. Everyone began talking, connecting relationships and telling family stories and anecdotes. A warm family feeling began to prevail.

Annabelle realized that Lexi was silent. "Lexi, tell us about yourself."

Lexi's eyes sparkled. "Well, I have an identical twin sister. We have great fun pretending to be each other. Even our parents can't tell us apart, so I pin an L on my shirt, and Ariel pins an A on hers. Andrew's roommate is in love with her, but we continually test him by switching letters. At this moment, as wonderfully close as Andrew and I are, he couldn't tell you if I were Lexi or Ariel."

Everyone applauded and laughed.

Carol held up her hands. "Listen, everybody. Next Sunday is Grandpa's birthday. We are invited to the Forester home to celebrate. I will call Sandy, but I know she would love for the four of you to attend and be a part of our family."

Annabelle, trying to hold back the tears of joy, answered, "We would also like to be a part of your family."

Charles looked at her. "By the way, Annabelle, where is Andrew's father?"

"Hello, Andrew. This is Edwin Rogers. Mrs. Forester instructed me to call you and offer you and Brad summer jobs in our Palm Beach law office after the way you handled yourself at the birthday party."

Andrew immediately called Annabelle. "Hello, Mother. Mr. Rogers just called and offered Brad and me summer jobs in his law office."

"That's great, Andrew."

Andrew then called his girlfriend. "Lexi, I just got offered a summer job at the Bailey and Forester law office along with Brad! That's great, especially since we have been discussing a future for me in politics. How does Senator and Mrs. Vanderbrook sound?"

"Honey," she whispered, "the sound of you making love to me would sound even better right now."

———◆———

Sandy called, "Randy honey, don't forget that we're meeting Dahlia and Tom for dinner tonight."

The server opened a bottle of the best house Merlot.

Sandy raised her glass. "Dear husbands, Dahlia and I are celebrating an important event. We are both pregnant and in our third month."

Both men gasped. "What happened?"

"Dahlia and I decided it was time to start a family, so we stopped taking the pills, and we became pregnant almost immediately. We realized, if we opened a discussion with you guys, there would always be reason to wait."

"Unbelievable!" was the startled response. "How did you know it would occur at the same time?"

"That was no problem, dear husbands. Every time we suggested we have sex, you guys were more than ready. Let's face the facts. You guys could screw us every night."

Tom spoke up, "Who could blame us to love the thrill of having great sex with the two most beautiful women in the world? It's a dream come true!"

"This is great news!" exclaimed Randy and Tom at the same time. "And we are very excited at the prospect of becoming fathers."

Randy looked at Sandy, always enthralled by her beauty.

His voice was choked with emotion, "Sweetheart, you have my heart, and I have yours. Together, we are starting a family."

Meanwhile Tom hugged Dahlia and whispered in her ear, "I love you, Dahlia Bailey. I love you with all my heart, and I am so happy that we're starting a family together."

Printed in the United States
By Bookmasters